# Crystal's Journey Home

## Crawdad Beach Series (Book 3)

Lisa Buffaloe

*Crystal's Journey Home*
John 15:11 Publications
Copyright 2024 Lisa Brewer Buffaloe
All rights reserved.

This novel is a work of fiction. Names, characters, places, towns, antique store owners, bakery owners, business owners, crawdads, dancing people, and all people and incidents are the product of the author's imagination and were used fictitiously. Any resemblance to actual events, persons living or dead, or any other person, including any place or thing, is entirely coincidental and beyond the author's intent.

Artificial Intelligence was not used in writing this book.

No crawdads were hurt in the writing of this novel.

Visit the author's website at https://lisabuffaloe.com.

ISBN: 978-1-957715-20-9 (eBook)
ISBN: 978-1-957715-19-3 (Paperback)
ISBN: 978-1-957715-21-6 (Hardcover)

Cover Design: JoAnn Durgin

## Table of Contents

# *Chapter 1*

## *Move to Crawdad Beach?*

Cell phone pressed to her ear; Crystal Baker kicked off her high heels as she considered what her sweet dad had just offered. Even though the idea was pleasant, she wasn't ready to make a move. However, she did promise her dad she'd pray about returning to her hometown since her relatives continued to shamelessly drop hints that she and her daughter needed to join them in Crawdad Beach. Crystal did miss her family, but she would never leave Olivia, and her daughter probably wouldn't leave her boyfriend, Geoff.

After saying goodbye to her dad, Crystal watched from the large front window of her home. Radio blaring, a car sped down the road, sending a flurry of trash airborne. The neighborhood had been well-maintained when she and her husband first married. Unfortunately, in the last couple of years, the area had declined.

If that wasn't bad enough, the hotel where she'd worked for the last seventeen years had just laid her off; the church where she was a member had sold their downtown property and moved to the suburbs; her favorite doctor had relocated his practice to Dallas, and her best friend had moved with her family to Fort Worth. Even her daughter's best friend had taken a job in Idaho.

Crystal shook her head. With all that was going on, her life sounded more and more like a bad country western song. Thank goodness her dog hadn't died. Not that she had one, but having a cute little pup around would be nice, like her dad's sweet dog, Filbert.

She turned away and focused on the photo of her late husband, Sean. They'd met in college, and the long, tall Texan had swept her off her feet. Their marriage had been wonderful until seven years ago when cancer cut short their plans for a long life together. The pain of Sean's absence wasn't as sharp as the first year, but she would always miss him.

Two years ago, she made the mistake of dating. The man's name was never to be mentioned by her or anyone who knew her. He had been attentive and sweet, and things seemed serious until she found out he was seriously dating another woman. Crystal groaned. She should never have tried to date anyone else because no one could come close to Sean. Plus, her dark brown hair now had a few streaks of gray, and although she tried to stay in shape, her figure wasn't the same as it had been in her twenties or thirties. She sucked in her stomach, and it still was a little bit poochy. Why couldn't people just get cuter as they aged?

Maybe she should have moved back to Crawdad Beach after Sean passed, but their daughter had been in high school at the time. If she'd uprooted Olivia then, her daughter would have had to leave the only home and friends she'd ever known. Olivia had been happy at school and with her church friends, but all that changed the first year after Sean died.

Crystal pressed her fingers against the bridge of her nose to stop her tears. If only she had known what she knew now, she would have packed them up and moved that first week. Things had gotten somewhat better, but Olivia's anger with God remained. She probably wouldn't even consider moving to a small town since she'd grown up in Houston's metropolis and had her own life working in one of the finest downtown restaurants.

Walking down the hall, Crystal stopped at her home office, turned on her computer, and checked her bank balance. She had a decent amount in savings and had received a fairly nice severance package, but how long would that last since she was only forty-five? Scrolling through the job sites, she sat back. She'd been in hotel management until a bigger chain bought them out and brought in their own team.

Starting over at her age and the level she'd been at her job would not be fun or easy, but what else could she do? She liked to read, but that didn't seem to be a paying occupation. She enjoyed making pottery but didn't have a kiln or workshop. Yardwork and gardening were fun, even if she constantly fought the thornbushes that came under the fence from the unkempt neighbor's yard. She made a fabulous salsa, but in Texas, most people seemed to have a salsa recipe.

She glanced around the room. Over the last couple of years, with the help of a carpenter friend, she'd renovated her house by updating the kitchen and bathrooms, painting the rooms, replacing the doors and windows, and adding new flooring to make it look like something seen on home improvement shows. Her friends told her she had skill in those areas, but who would want to hire a forty-something widow for construction work?

No matter what she chose as her next step, change was coming. Crystal pushed out of her chair, turned on the music app on her cell phone, and danced to her favorite song. When she was nervous, needed to think, or just wanted some exercise, she danced. Her family told her she absolutely had no sense of rhythm, yet in her mind, she was poetry in motion.

After the song ended, Crystal rubbed her throbbing hip. Dancing irritated the hip, and lately, walking did, too. Sometimes, at night, it felt like her hip was going out of joint. Hopefully, she wouldn't need a hip replacement like her dad. Surely not. She'd probably just tweaked something.

What she did need was salsa. The healing properties of salsa always made her feel better. Limping to the kitchen, she grabbed a bag of tortilla chips and two jars of her homemade salsa. Maybe she'd even go for three. Since she was no longer employed and had no idea what was next, she might put away the chips and guzzle straight from the jars.

Eric Reed reviewed Doohickeys Hardware sales information for the day and then shut down his computer. The building's old wood floors creaked as he made a final pass to ensure the store was empty before locking up for the night. He hesitated as he stood at the front door and glanced at the deep, rich wood shelving filled with old and new items. The store had been in his family since 1916 and passed from generation to generation. If something didn't sell, they still kept the item because you never knew what someone might need for a home improvement project.

He loved managing Doohickeys, but after work, going home to an empty house just stunk. Amy, his late wife, had died over two years ago, and it still didn't seem real. He thought they would be one of those couples married for seventy-plus years; instead, Leukemia had taken her before she turned forty-two. Since both of their daughters were away at college, he didn't have a reason to go home.

Maybe he should get a dog. Should he get something big and tough or small and lap size? As a single guy, he didn't want one of those primpy pups that needed grooming every few days. He wanted a wash-and-wear dog that didn't shed too much. Did they even make canines like that?

He locked up the store, then strolled down the sidewalk next to the brick-paved main street. Crawdad Beach was growing and undergoing positive changes, bringing in more customers than ever for his store. He walked past Curl and Dye Beauty Salon, the law office, the two buildings converted to loft apartments, and stopped at Tiddlywinks Restaurant. As he entered, the owners greeted him with a smile and wave.

Since Eric had grown up in Crawdad Beach, most of the townspeople were more like family than friends. He sat at a table in the back and glanced at the menu that featured a cartoon crawdad wearing a chef's hat. Amy and his girls used to imagine the tiny crustacean lived in the kitchen and cooked all the food.

Couples and families around him sat enjoying their meals, and here he was sitting alone again. He didn't mind most days, but for some weird reason, today, he seemed even lonelier. Before Amy died, she'd done her best to prepare him and their daughters. But still, the grief that first year had been hard, thick, and depressing. He still missed Amy, but his fog seemed to have lifted.

Life kept moving on even when he didn't want to keep going. God had been gracious not to strike him dead when Eric screamed and shook his fist at Him for taking Amy. Even in his anger, questions, and hurt, he'd found the God of all comfort in the worst time of his life.

"Hi, Mr. Eric." Jennifer, the curly-haired brunette with big brown eyes, held a small pad and pen as she stopped beside his table. "What can I get you today?"

"The usual, please."

She grinned. "Chicken, green beans, mashed potatoes, and cobbler, right?"

"That's right. Thanks. So, how's married life?"

Jennifer's smile widened. "It's great. We've been married three years now."

"Good for you." He smiled at her excitement. "Enjoy one another."

She nodded with enthusiasm. "Oh, I have, and I will."

After she left, Eric sat back in his chair. He missed married life. Amy had made him promise he would remarry, but he shuddered at the thought of dating again. Besides Amy, his high school sweetheart was the only other girl he would have considered marrying, but that was years ago, and last he heard, she was living in another state.

He'd lived in Crawdad Beach all his life and started working at Doohickeys as soon as he could stand. What woman would want to marry a guy without a college degree who owned a hardware store? He definitely needed a dog—someone to keep him company at night.

Next week, he'd drive to the shelter and see what they had available. If lucky, he'd find one already house-trained and ready for a long-term relationship.

# *Chapter 2*

At seven a.m., Henry Doss groaned as he got out of bed and struggled to get on his knees. Now that he was older, his body didn't care much for the position, but his soul desperately needed to talk to God. His little dog, Filbert, knelt next to Henry with paws in front as though joining in prayer.

Henry patted his furry friend and turned his attention back to why he was kneeling. In addition to praying for his daughter, Crystal, and all that was going on in her life, Henry was also concerned about his granddaughter, Olivia. She was dating one of the chefs in the cooking competition Henry had watched on television last night. His granddaughter's boyfriend, Geoff, had shamelessly flirted with the other female contestants, and Henry believed there would be trouble ahead for his precious Olivia.

She had rebelled after Sean died and had turned from God. He'd prayed for years for Olivia's return to God's loving arms. Olivia knew God had even been baptized as a young girl, but she'd chosen to walk away from God, the church, and her church friends. Olivia might run from

God, but she couldn't outrun God's love or the many prayers prayed on her behalf.

Henry prayed and prayed some more for Olivia, Crystal, and all his family. An idea and several Bible verses confirmed what Henry was considering. Were the thoughts his own or God's guidance? Henry opened his Bible to read, study, and pray some more. Then, he knew without a doubt what he was supposed to do.

Thanking God, Henry rose to his feet and placed a call to his other daughter, Katherine. After their conversation, he ate a quick breakfast. He needed to get downtown to finalize his ideas for the latest Crawdad Beach renovation project.

Henry let Filbert outside for a few moments. Once his little dog returned, Henry patted him on the head and explained that he would be home soon. Filbert gave him a thoughtful look, wagged, and then curled up on his dog bed. Some people thought talking to their animals didn't make sense, but Henry believed Filbert understood more than most canines.

He texted his granddaughter-in-love, Marie, to let her know where he was going. His grandson David and his wife Marie were kind enough to add on to their house and give Henry his own private quarters.

Taking his cane, he hurried out the entrance of the addition where he lived. Although his family thought he always needed to carry his cane, he really didn't need it.

However, in the past, the brass-topped wooden cane had come in handy in more ways than for walking.

The trees, just starting to show their fall color, lined the sidewalk as he made his way downtown. Ever since Crawdad Beach had been featured in a popular home magazine a few months ago, the businesses along Main Street stayed busier than ever. The tourist trade was always welcome in their small town, but he did miss the quiet days of his childhood.

Henry walked along the sidewalk beside the brick-paved main street. A horn beeped, and he turned to wave. The police chief shouted a greeting as he drove his car slowly past.

Stopping in front of Knick Knack's Antique Store, Henry peeked in the front windows. The owner, Jeremy, and his wife, Grace, stood behind the counter, smiling at one another. They hadn't been married long and still had that dreamy-eyed look. When they spotted him, they smiled and waved. Henry returned the greeting, then glanced heavenward and thanked God for the many answered prayers for those young ones. Now, he prayed God would be gracious again to help with his family.

"Good morning, Mr. Doss."

"Good morning, Alexa." He chuckled as the former track star, still sporting a lightning bolt shaved in her dark hair, power-walked past him.

Stepping up his gait, Henry moved on and entered the old two-story brick building that his daughter, Katherine, was renovating. He watched her as she stood on a ladder removing old wiring. Her dark hair and beautiful big brown eyes made her look so much like his late wife. Thankfully, all his children had a touch of his wife's Asian beauty.

"Been looking for treasure?"

"Hi, Dad." Katherine stepped off the ladder and turned his way. "I don't think we'll find anything here like they did at Knick Knacks, but I did find a 1930 newspaper under the floorboards, an old shoe, and some old pennies." She approached him as she wiped her hands on a rag. "Are you sure you want to do this?"

Henry nodded. "Yes, let me buy the building from you, and you can continue the renovation for me."

Katherine gave him a curious smile. "Dad, what are you planning?"

He stood taller, firm in his convictions. "I want it prepared for Crystal and Olivia."

"My sister, Crystal, and her daughter, Olivia, who both love living in Texas?" Katherine's expression said she wasn't sure they would ever leave Houston.

"Yes." Henry tapped his cane on the floor. "I want you to build a nice apartment on the top floor with two bedrooms and two bathrooms and then have the wiring ready downstairs for a coffee shop or a bakery. Wire it in case they want big ovens, coffee machines, or whatever else they need."

"Dad, what are you not telling me? Renovating like that will be expensive. I don't mind completing the building at my cost. It's what I love doing. I've already started working on the upstairs apartment and preparing it for a tenant."

"You always do a great job, but please let me pay for this one. I still have money in savings and a tidy sum from selling my house, and I have very few expenses. Crystal has been a widow for seven years, and she needs to move here so we can care for her and Olivia."

Katherine chuckled as she shook her head. "Crystal is forty-five and younger than I am." She tilted her head as she surveyed him. "Wait, what do you know that I don't know?"

"They both need a fresh start, and it's time. Besides, Crystal just got laid off from her job."

"What? Oh, man, that's tough." Katherine's shoulders drooped as she shook her head. "I talked to her last week, and she said they were having layoffs after the other hotel chain bought them out, but I didn't think it would touch her."

"Unfortunately, the new company is bringing in their own management. Crystal just found out the other day."

"Then, you're right." Katherine gave him a quick nod. "We need to do this. I'm on board, especially since you seem to have a hotline to God. And you've helped all your kids and grandkids over the years, especially in prayer. Let's sit down, and I'll give you some preliminary figures.

But you do know, Crystal won't leave Olivia." She motioned for him to follow her to the staircase.

"I know." Henry sat beside her on the steps. "That's why I want you to get the building ready."

Katherine cocked her head. "So, you think because offering a business like Aunt Helen did with her great-nephew Jeremy, that Crystal and Olivia will be open to moving here if you have a ready-made business for them?"

Henry nodded. "I prayed and believe this is the right thing for both of them."

"Okay." Katherine took her laptop and showed Henry the figures for the building's purchase and renovation costs. "Since Crystal did a great job renovating her entire house, maybe she would want to come help me with this project."

"I like that idea. I think she'd enjoy that. When you were little girls, you two were always working on building something."

Katherine's eyes glazed in pleasure. "Yeah, not too many girls were more interested in tools than playing with dolls."

"You did build the best tree fort in the area."

Katherine nudged him. "Do you remember the morning when Crystal had been in the bathroom and she walked past all of us sitting at the breakfast table and came back a few minutes later carrying a big wrench? Not anyone said anything to her. She walked past us all, and then we could hear her grunting, groaning, and pounding on a pipe. A few minutes later, Crystal walked out with the wrench again and put it away."

Henry chuckled at the memory. "I remember. That was when she had been getting ready for school, and her ring fell down the drain. She removed the plumbing and found it still in the sink trap."

"She could do just about anything, couldn't she?"

"Yes, she could. Go ahead and call Crystal and ask if she would be willing to help you with the renovation." Henry tapped his chin as he considered. "If you call her, remind her what a great place Crawdad Beach would be for both of them. She needs to come home, and Olivia needs to be here."

"Sounds like a plan." Katherine stood and helped Henry to his feet. "She can stay at my house while we work. And hopefully, Olivia will also join her."

"I pray so. I'm not fond of who she's dating."

"I agree. I saw the cooking show that Geoff is on. He may be a great chef, but Olivia could do much better for a boyfriend. She had been thrilled for him, but the way he acted around the other women, he's..." Katherine shook her head. "I won't say what I think he is. Let's make sure and see if we can't get Crystal and Olivia here."

"Good. I'll be over at Tiddlywinks. Call me if you need anything." Henry hugged his daughter, then hurried across the street and entered the crowded restaurant. His stomach growled at the smell of bacon, eggs, fresh-brewed coffee, and the other pleasant scents surrounding him. Spotting the owner, Faith Hollis, Henry waved to catch her attention.

The sweet, short, round woman with silver hair and plump cheeks hurried his way. "Henry, what are you doing here this morning?"

Keeping his focus on her, he motioned toward the line of people. "Faith, do you have a moment?"

"For you, yes." She grinned as she led him back to the small office in the back. "I can tell by the twinkle in your blue eyes you are up to something."

"You would be right."

Faith's husband, George, sat behind a big oak desk. The big man looked up and grinned. "Hey, Henry. Good to see you."

"Good to see you, too." Henry shook the man's outstretched hand and sat across from the couple. "I'm sure you know that Katherine is working on another building."

"She does such a great job," Faith said.

Her husband, George, nodded. "Your daughter has a real talent, Henry."

Henry smiled at them both. "Yes, I agree. The one Katherine's working on might become a coffee shop offering pastries or maybe a bakery. I hope to convince my daughter Crystal and my granddaughter Olivia to move here."

"Crystal might move back?" Faith's smile beamed. "How exciting. I always loved her. She's such a sweetie."

Henry sat taller in his chair. "Her daughter, Olivia, is a pastry chef in Houston, and she's also been one of the coffee shop people."

"You mean, a Barista? George asked.

"Yes, that's it." Henry nodded. "Katherine is preparing the building to be ready for them. I was wondering if you would be willing to answer any questions they might have about running a business in Crawdad Beach. I would pay for your time and trouble. What do you think?"

"Goodness, there's no need to pay us." Faith waved a dismissive hand his way. "We will be glad to help in any way possible."

"You bet." George nodded and smiled. "They are more than welcome to call us for anything."

"Thank you," Henry stood. "Since you're both praying people, would you pray for God's best for all concerned? Either way, I've told Katherine to prepare the building, and I will also alert the Crawdad Beach prayer team."

Faith's face beamed as she rose and came next to him. "This will be so much fun. I love watching God work."

"Hey, what's going on in here?" Grinning, Chester Taylor stood at the office door.

After everyone greeted Chester, Henry said goodbye to the Hollis's and motioned for Chester to follow him outside. Once they were on the sidewalk, Henry explained everything to his best friend.

"This is great," Chester said. "Another adventure for the Crawdadians."

"I don't want the whole town to know," Henry said in a low voice, "but I will send information to the prayer group."

Chester rubbed his hands together. "I've got extra time since Grace now works more hours at Knick Knacks. Since she married Jeremy, that girl practically glows. Plus, she doesn't wear her glasses anymore, and her long brown hair falls free around her shoulders. It's great to see her so happy."

"God was good to bring Jeremy and Grace together."

"That's for sure," Chester said with a smiling nod. "So, back to the building renovation. How can I help?"

"Well, if Crystal and Olivia open a coffee and pastry shop-type place, they'll need tables for the customers. Jeremy and Grace's antique store should be a good place to locate furniture for the new business."

"Great idea. We could strike up a deal with Jeremy. And, I could get Maybelline and Helen to join me in looking for bistro-type tables when we're on our outings to buy for Knick Knacks."

"Excellent," Henry agreed. "Let's talk to Jeremy first, then call your wife and my sister. I'm praying that this isn't just something I want. I do desire and pray the best for Crystal and Olivia."

"I understand. I'll join in prayer, and we'll have fun moving forward with projects until we see what happens."

Chester stayed in step beside Henry as they walked down the sidewalk. "By the way, I saw the cooking show the other night with that guy Olivia is dating. Geoff might be the chef in one of those Michelin restaurants. But who cares if he sells tires? That doesn't mean he can cook."

Chuckling, Henry stopped and shook his head. "No, the Michelin Star is for restaurants with outstanding cooking."

"Oh, I sure was wondering why everyone was all woo-woo about that." He waved his hand around. "Well, I don't care if Geoff cooks, sells tires, or what he does. Olivia needs someone who treats her right."

# *Chapter 3*

Even as the little dog wagged, her tail crooked to one side at a forty-five-degree angle. Eric knelt in front of a cage at the animal shelter and stared at the little black, brown, and white puppy. He glanced up at the young, dark-haired volunteer. "Is her tail okay?"

"We think so," she said with a shrug. "It's probably just a birth defect."

Eric rubbed his chin. He shouldn't be considering a dog that wasn't fully grown, but he was drawn to the little pup that looked as lonely as he felt. "Where did she come from?"

"A lady found her wandering in the woods over by the lake. The puppy was just about starving. We aren't sure if the mom abandoned her or if something else happened. Either way, she's been here for over a week, and no one has claimed her. We've also searched the internet to see if anyone is missing a little dog. Nothing turned up. Let me get her out, and you can see what you think." She opened the cage door, and the pup ran to Eric's arms. The volunteer grinned. "Looks like she's ready to go home with you."

Eric cuddled the soft, little wiggling dog against his chest. "I don't know. I was thinking of a bigger one, a little older, something already house-trained and not one that sheds too much."

"She might be little now, but we think she'll probably be about twenty-five pounds. Perfect for companionship. As for shedding, she shouldn't shed too much based on her fur type. And any training shouldn't take too long."

The puppy licked Eric's hand and gazed longingly into his eyes. He could imagine his girls would love to see a little dog when they came home on their Thanksgiving and Christmas breaks. And it would be nice to have someone staring adoringly at him. It had been years since he'd owned a dog. If he did take this one with him, since he lived only two blocks from Doohickeys, he could always come home during the day to check on her.

He huffed out a breath. The little dog stared up at him and huffed right back. Eric laughed and rubbed her soft fur. "Okay, tell me what I need to do, and I'll take her home."

Propped in her bed, Crystal leaned against her pillow and studied the information the real estate agent had given her. The changes and upgrades Crystal had made to her little house would pay off if she decided to put it on the market. Thankfully, the neighborhood sale prices were still reasonable since house flippers were buying up property around her street to renovate. Her improvements had just beat them to the punch.

If she did sell her house, she'd have a nice nest egg for the future. Of course, she'd have to find another place to live, and she had no clue where to go or what to do. Her sister, Katherine, had called earlier to offer an opportunity to help renovate an old building. Crystal grinned. Spending a couple of weeks playing with tools and visiting family sounded like a nice getaway.

She'd been praying about moving back to Crawdad Beach, but if she did, she didn't know what she could do in the small town. Plenty of hotels were closer to the beach; maybe they had openings where she could work. Crystal grabbed her laptop, opened the online job sites, and checked what was available. No one needed her level of experience. However, if she didn't mind taking a significant pay cut, there were plenty of opportunities. She bit back a laugh. Pay cut? Her salary was currently at zero dollars. Anything would be an improvement.

The bigger question, however, was, could she leave Texas? The thought of leaving her daughter was gut-wrenching, but what if moving to Crawdad Beach was what Crystal needed to do? The more she prayed about possibly returning to her hometown, the stronger her urge to move to South Carolina. But was it because most things in her life had changed, or were they changing to help her make that decision? Her legs started twitching, itching for dance relief.

Her cell signaled an incoming text from Olivia. Crystal read the message. No time for dancing now. She put on her robe, grabbed her laptop, and hurried to wait on the couch. It might be eleven o'clock at night, but it didn't matter. Her daughter needed to talk and was on her way over. Maybe she could convince Olivia it was time to step out into the great unknown.

Thirty minutes later, after listening to her daughter's troubles with her crummy boyfriend. Crystal tried not to say too much. She never liked Geoff. He was an egotistical man who seemed to think more highly of himself than anyone else. Her daughter didn't need to waste any more time with someone who didn't cherish her.

Crystal put her arm around Olivia's shoulder. "I'm sorry. I know you're hurting."

"I don't know what to do." Olivia groaned. "Geoff only called me two times when he was in California. Mom, he called the restaurant every day, sometimes several times. Then, watching him flirt with the other female contestants on the show was like I didn't even exist. Plus, I overheard him talking to a friend this morning who was joking about Geoff's flirting with the women on the show. His friend even asked about me because he thought we were an item. Geoff just laughed and said I was *only* a pastry chef." Olivia's big brown eyes shimmered with unshed tears.

"Ouch. I'm sorry." Crystal's heart hurt for her girl. Olivia looked like Sean, tall and slim with light brown hair and big brown eyes. She could do so much better than Geoff.

"Mom, we've dated a long time." Olivia fisted her hands. "I thought our relationship was getting serious, but watching how he acted with the other women, now I wonder what I've been thinking. And you know what else? When Geoff noticed I was upset, he got mad at *me* and told me I should be happy for him because this show was his big break."

Crystal bit her tongue from saying what she wanted to say about Geoff. Instead, she patted her daughter's shoulder. "Oh honey, I'm sorry. Maybe he's showing his true colors."

"Yeah, and the colors are not pretty." Olivia shoved off the couch and paced back and forth. "I'm sick of Geoff, sick of working in the same restaurant with him. I knew he was a flirt, but I tried to ignore it, thinking he was just being friendly with customers because of the business. Now, I realize he's just a flirt."

"I'm sorry, honey." Crystal waited a moment. Should she say what she was thinking about and praying about? Maybe she'd put out a feeler and see if Olivia would consider moving. "Maybe it's time for a change, a move to somewhere new."

"You mean in the suburbs?"

Crystal shook her head. "No, maybe out of state."

"Out of state?" Olivia stopped pacing. "Why would we do that? We love Texas."

"True, but I've been laid off."

Olivia sunk on the couch next to her. "Why didn't you tell me?"

"I didn't want to say anything while you have your own problems. It's only been a few days since they let me go."

"Mom, we're in this together. I mean, I know I have my own apartment. But, we're family. You should have told me."

Crystal shrugged. "Well, I just told you. Your Aunt Katherine's renovating an old building in downtown Crawdad Beach and wanted to know if we'd come help."

"Renovating?" Olivia cut her eyes at her. "That's stuff you like to do."

"True. But Katherine's making an apartment on the top floor and turning the bottom one into a coffee shop, bakery, or combination of the two. She thought you would have some great ideas since you're in the restaurant business. Plus, it would allow us both to get away and figure out what we want to do next. You haven't taken a vacation in over a year, and now I have lots of time. Plus, we could see my dad and my family. It would be nice to get away. Will you think about it? Better yet, would you pray about what's next for you and me? Please." Since she was rambling, Crystal stopped saying anything else and prayed the ideas would percolate positively in her daughter's brain.

Olivia sat quietly as differing emotions flickered across her face. "I guess it would be nice to see Grandad and the family. I always loved the little town."

"I hear it's growing. Last month, Katherine finished converting the second old building into loft apartments." Crystal took her laptop and opened the webpage for the completed buildings. "Check out the photos."

Olivia gazed at the website. "Those are nice. I love the wood floors, brick walls, and beamed ceilings. I couldn't afford anything like that here in Houston."

"Katherine's preparing the first floor of the building for a business, then making the top floor into a two-bedroom, two-bath apartment with a laundry room, den, dining area, kitchen, and fireplace. It will also have French Doors leading to a balcony overlooking Main Street."

"That sounds nice. I'm impressed." Olivia's eyes narrowed as she gazed her way. "Wait, you sound like you want to move and stay there."

"It's a thought." Crystal tried to act semi-innocent. "I've been praying about it."

"I'm sure you have." Olivia looked disgusted, then moved her eyebrows upward. "But if you moved away..." Her bottom lip trembled. "What would I do?"

Crystal hugged her tight. "I don't know for sure that I'll go yet, but the more I've prayed about it, the more I've felt the prompting to go back to Crawdad Beach."

"But, you grew up there. I don't have any friends that live in that area."

"I would be there, and you would have the support of all our Crawdadian relatives."

"I don't know. Relocating is a big thing." Olivia pulled back from the embrace. "If we moved there, what would I do? It's a nice place, but it's just a small town."

"Well, besides the building my sister is renovating, there are lots of work opportunities closer to the beach. We don't have to decide anything right now. We could go there for a week or so, and you could help with demolition to relieve some frustration." Crystal silently prayed for God to nudge her daughter to go with her.

Olivia rose and walked to the front window. For a long time, she didn't say anything, just stared out at the darkness. She sighed long and slow, but her lips quirked in a grin as she turned toward her. "I'll go with you and help with the demolition, but only if I get to use dynamite."

"I'm not sure about that, but some good old-fashioned sledgehammers might do the trick." Crystal pulled up the flight information she already had saved on her computer. "I have enough frequent flyer miles for both of us. Why don't you let me know what works best for your schedule, and I'll make the arrangements?"

Olivia let out a big breath as her gaze dropped to the floor. She stood quiet for a moment, then looked her way.

"I can tell you right now. Let's plan on going next week. I need to get away from Geoff. The sooner, the better."

# Chapter 4

**D**oohickeys' longtime employee, Gloria, pointed to the spreadsheet. "We've had a great month. Business has picked up with the added tourist trade."

"It has been great." Eric smiled at Gloria. She wore slacks and a cobalt blue top that looked great with her milk chocolate complexion and sparkling brown eyes. He stifled a chuckle that he even noticed and knew the hue of blue was cobalt. His daughters would be proud.

Eric surveyed the work she had done. "I appreciate all that you do for us. I sure couldn't run the place without you." Gloria had worked at the hardware store for thirty-five years and probably knew as much, or more, about the business as he did. She had a business degree, was in charge of accounting and purchasing, and could handle anything and everything needed to run the store.

"Probably not." Gloria smiled his way. "But, you know that's not true. I'm grateful God opened the door to work here all those years ago. It's been a blessing."

"We've been through a lot together, haven't we?" Eric sat back in his chair. Gloria had watched him grow from a little squirt of a kid to managing the store. She'd rejoiced at his marriage and the birth of his daughters, then prayed and comforted him through the loss of his dad, mom, and wife.

"We have been through quite a lot," Gloria said, her smile falling and rebounding. "God got us through the hard stuff, and he will get us through whatever's next." Gloria also knew her share of heartache. She'd lost a son in Afghanistan, and her husband had to retire early due to heart problems.

Eric nodded. "I would like to place a vote that we don't have any more hard stuff."

"I will vote the same, but you know that's not likely what will happen. We are still on a journey through enemy territory until God calls us home. Our momentary, light affliction is producing for us an eternal weight of glory far beyond all comparison."

He smiled at the scripture verse. "Sometimes that light affliction is very heavy."

"Yes, it is. But nothing compares to what is next for us in the glorious eternity with Christ."

"You're right. Thanks, Gloria. You're the best." He stood. "I'm going to run home and check on my pup."

"Take your time. Sammie and I will keep a watch on things."

Eric grinned as he walked out of the store. He had great employees. Besides Gloria, Sammie had been working at Doohickeys for three years. He'd started working when he turned sixteen after his school days ended. After graduating high school, Sammie began working full-time at the store, determined to stay in Crawdad Beach since his lineage went back to the first settlers. Plus, his parents lived here and were organic farmers, good people, not wealthy, who lived simply and embraced life to the fullest.

Eric hurried to his car. He could walk to his place but wanted to get home and check on Gadget. He thought about calling the little pup something more feminine, but he was a guy, and a guy didn't need a foo-foo name for his dog. Doohickeys Hardware was known for offering any doohickey or whatchamacallit needed for any project, so what would be better than having a dog named Gadget?

A few minutes later, Eric unlocked the door at his house. The pup, with a toy in her mouth, wagging like crazy, came running toward him. He scooped her in his arms and rubbed her soft fur as he checked around the room to ensure Gadget hadn't had any accidents. Fortunately, she'd been a good girl. He took her outside for a quick potty break. When finished, Gadget bounced around in the grass, exploring the backyard. They'd only been together two weeks, but she'd already brightened his life.

When he video-called his girls to show them Gadget, they were both thrilled about the puppy but unhappy with the name Eric had chosen for her. Since her tail had that forty-five-degree angle, they would have preferred her to be named Angleina. But that sounded too much like

Angelina, and he figured people would stumble over that. Gadget might not be a feminine name, but the pup seemed okay with it.

He called her and led her back inside. After ensuring her water dish was filled, he gave Gadget a belly rub and a treat, and then he headed back to work.

As he drove down Main Street, he slowed to check the progress of the building under renovation. Katherine was his best high-dollar client. He appreciated she would come to him first to get supplies when she could order things herself or use the big home improvement stores closer to the beach.

Whenever Katherine came into Doohickeys, if there was an out-of-towner, they were surprised to learn she was a builder since Henry Doss sure had beautiful women for his daughters. Eric smiled at the thought of Henry's youngest, Crystal. They had been friends in high school and even dated. Once she married, she moved to Texas, and although a widow, she still lived there. Hopefully, she was doing well.

Eric parked his car and stepped back into his store. He didn't regret a moment of his time with his late wife, Amy, but now that he was single again, he sure wished Crystal had stayed in Crawdad Beach.

At the blinking red light, Crystal stopped her rental car and grinned at the sign with a cute cartoon crawfish welcoming people to Crawdad Beach. The tension she didn't even know she'd been carrying uncoiled the tightened muscles of her neck. She'd missed being home.

The hours spent on the flight from Texas gave her time to think and pray about moving. The closer they'd gotten to South Carolina, the stronger the urge to sell her house and relocate. Plus, when they landed at the airport, a very tempting message had come from the realtor back in Texas.

Driving on, Crystal passed the gas station, the volunteer fire department, the white-steepled church and crossed the unused railroad tracks.

"I love the cartoon crawdad." Olivia pointed to the mural of the crawdad sitting on a beach reading a book that graced the side of the public library in the old railroad depot.

"Me too. Your cousin Tess painted those for the town."

"That's right, I had forgotten about that. Tess is really talented."

"She is." Crystal drove past Mitchell's Grocery Store and motioned with her chin to the building. "Your cousin David is now the full-time manager."

"Did Uncle Michael finally retire?"

"Yes and no. He sometimes works at the store but also helps Katherine with her projects. Plus, they take fun road trips now and then."

"You know, it's strange that Tess and David are married, and they both have twins. Since we're related, would that mean I could have twins if I got pregnant?" A panicked look crossed Olivia's face.

Crystal's heartbeat rocketed. "Pregnant?"

Olivia gave her a disgusted look. "I'm not talking about now. I'm not pregnant or anything. I'm just saying if I had kids, I'd need to start with just one and make sure I knew what I was getting into."

Crystal chuckled. "I don't think you get to decide, plus I don't think any parent knows what they are getting into with children. It's always interesting." She slowed her speed as she drove down the brick-paved main street. Renovations and upgrades on the two-story brick buildings made the town look even cuter than when they'd been here at Christmas.

She glanced at her daughter. "Crawdad Beach was a great place to live, and now it's even better. Just think how many relatives live here. And your grandad still has the lake house with jet skis. We'll have to go over one day and hang out."

Olivia grabbed her arm. "Mom, slow up. I see Lawnmower Lucy."

Crystal took her foot off the accelerator. Sure enough, Lucy, wearing a purple velveteen jogging suit, was hunched down in racing position as she putted along on her pink racing-stripped lawnmower toward them on Main Street.

They both waved at the woman who once had been a champion lawnmower racer.

"Isn't she like ninety years old?" Olivia asked.

"I don't think anyone knows her age, but she's not giving up riding her mower around town. Thank goodness her son removed the blades and throttled down the engine."

Crystal continued driving through the downtown area and slowed to where the road curved around the community park. Even though it was fall, flowers and crepe myrtles were still blooming. She stopped the car in the parking area by the historical marker that stated Crawdad Beach had been established in 1881. The name had come from one of the children who had noticed a crawdad sunning on the sandy riverbank.

Olivia cast a questioning gaze in her direction. "Why are we stopping?"

"We had some happy times when we visited here when you were a little girl." Crystal leaned over the steering wheel.

"We did." Olivia nodded. "Dad loved this little park."

"Sean was a kid at heart. I'm grateful for our time with him, but I would have preferred it had been much longer. He will always be a sweet spot in both our lives." Smiling at the memories, Crystal sighed. Their little family used to stroll on the path beside the small sandy river, often stopping to sit by a longstanding cypress tree. "Maybe we can walk by the river a few times while we're here."

"I still miss him." Olivia's eyes shimmered in tears. "It wasn't fair." Her words were only a whisper.

Crystal gave a gentle pat on her daughter's arm. She'd prayed and prayed for Olivia, but a simmering just-below-the-surface anger remained.

Praying and wishing things were different, Crystal pulled back onto the road. "Let's go see what your Aunt Katherine is up to." Returning downtown, she parked in front of the building her sister was renovating.

After exiting the car, Crystal rubbed her sore hip as she stopped outside the door and admired the building's woodwork. "Look how beautiful. The millwork is amazing, isn't it? You don't see craftsmanship like that anymore."

"It is pretty." Olivia's gaze traveled up and down the street. "Did you notice how busy the town is today?"

"Lots of tourists come to Crawdad Beach. Dad said the town had been written up in a popular home magazine about being a great place to visit." Entering the building, Crystal stopped. Demolition was further along than she had realized. The brick walls were exposed, and the old hardwood floors and tin ceiling gave it an old-world look. "This is nice. I can see so much potential."

The sound of hammering came from the floor above.

Olivia pushed her forward. "Aunt Katherine must be working upstairs."

Crystal followed her daughter up the staircase. As they stepped inside the apartment door, they both stopped and stared at the high ceilings, exposed beams, and ductwork painted black. A stone fireplace sat on the back wall, and large windows let in plenty of natural light.

"Wow, you've been busy." Crystal hurried to hug her big sister.

"Hey, you two. I'm so glad you're here." Katherine hugged them both and motioned like a game show host with her hand. "What do you think?"

"It's nice." Crystal glanced at the kitchen. Custom cabinets and countertops were in the process of being installed. "I can't believe you've gotten so much done already."

Katherine smiled at the men working in the kitchen. "I have a great work crew. I hope to finish the upstairs in a week or two. The downstairs still needs lots of work."

"Mom told me you might make it a coffee shop or bakery," Olivia said.

"That's right. Come on, I'd like your advice." Katherine led them to the main floor and turned to Olivia. "Since you know the restaurant business, what would I need to install to get it ready for a bakery or a coffee shop that sells pastries? We have enough tourist trade that someone could have a profitable business here. Plus, most of our town has a sweet tooth."

Olivia gazed around at the empty shell on the first floor. "Well, you'd need a kitchen with the proper equipment, counters for coffee and supplies, a counter for display and service, a couple of bathrooms for the clients, an office for the owner, and a storage area. You might not need as many supplies or employees if the building is mainly a bakery. Most people who just want coffee would probably prefer a drive-through, and there's no way to do that here."

"Good points. We'll have to think further about all of those logistics. Maybe the building is better suited as a bakery." Katherine motioned for them to follow toward the rear of the building and opened a door revealing a loading dock. "I'm planning on enclosing this to turn part into a storage area and making the rest a garage for the owner so they can park out of the rain and have privacy. I've already input some ideas into my computer design software." She turned to Olivia. "Would you be willing to help me map out what would be needed? I haven't ever been involved in this kind of thing before, so having you here is a real blessing."

"Sure," Olivia said. "That sounds fun."

Katherine turned to Crystal. "And, I'd love your help on design ideas since you were involved in the hotel business, and you know what makes things look hospitable for clients."

"You got it," Crystal said. "We also hoped to help with the renovation's manual labor."

Katherine grinned. "I'll be glad to take you up on that offer."

"We have work clothes in our suitcases," Olivia said. "Should we change here or go somewhere else?"

"Here would be fine. The bathrooms upstairs will give privacy." Katherine pointed toward the stairs.

When Olivia left to get their luggage, Katherine moved closer to Crystal. "So, do you think you'll stay?"

Crystal gave her sister a hopeful nod. "The minute I drove into town, I felt like it's where I belong, but if Olivia stays in Texas, it will be hard to leave her behind. Thanks for making us both feel welcome."

"Of course. I hope we can tempt you both to move here soon. Dad and the rest of the family are praying." Katherine checked the time. "I'll text him to let him know you're in town."

After they changed clothing, Olivia and Katherine sat together to discuss what would be needed to prepare the building, as Crystal made a few minor suggestions.

Her dad entered the building with a big smile on his face. "I'm so glad you're both here." He hurried toward them and hugged them all before addressing Olivia. "What do you think about the project?"

"It's really nice, Granddad. It's going to be fun to be part of the process."

"We were hoping you would find it enjoyable. I'm sure you have some great ideas for the building. Tell

Katherine everything you'd like to have if you were running the business."

Olivia gazed back and forth at them all, then crossed her arms. "Wait, are y'all thinking what I'm thinking?"

Crystal gave her an innocent look. "What would you think we're thinking?"

Olivia's mouth opened and then closed. "I think you all have plans," she huffed, "and I haven't made any plans... yet."

Crystal smiled reassuringly at her daughter. "No worries. We've got time to play and help with the renovation."

Dad moved closer to Olivia, "We would love to have you both stay here. The building is free of charge for you and your mom."

Olivia stared at them all wide-eyed. "What are you saying? For us?" She stared at them for a moment and shook her head. "That's very nice of you, but I have a life back in Texas. I... I can't move."

"Why not?" Crystal sent up desperate prayers for help that Olivia wouldn't shut down or shut them out.

"I have a job and...." Olivia's gaze dropped to the floor. "I just can't leave."

"Why not? You could have your own business here."

Olivia frowned and held up her hands. "At least give me some time to think about this. I just thought we would live in Texas forever."

"I understand." Crystal came beside Olivia. "But, maybe it's time for a new beginning. Both of us could use some fun and adventure. You don't have to decide right now. Please don't worry. Let's just have fun and enjoy being together with family."

Olivia sighed as she walked to the big front windows and gazed outside. "Crawdad Beach is a cute little town. But Mom, what would you do if I stayed in Texas?"

Crystal's stomach churned at the thought as she came next to her daughter. "I'm not sure. Either way, I'm selling the house. The realtor called and has a very nice cash offer from a potential buyer."

"I didn't know you had it listed."

"I didn't, but the realtor knew I was considering selling. He said he had someone looking in that area ready to buy."

"But, where would you go?" Olivia sounded like a little girl.

Crystal put her arm around her daughter's shoulder. "That's part of why we're here. I feel drawn back to my hometown, but I don't know if it's because I loved growing up here or if it's my next step. Whatever I decide, I want to ensure you are okay."

"I'm an adult. I'll be fine." Olivia straightened her back, but her eyes held a level of doubt.

"You're an adult, but you're my only child. If you don't feel like leaving Texas and want me with you, I'll figure out something and stay there, too."

"I don't want you to make decisions based on me alone." Olivia gazed back out of the window. "I wish I could peek into the future to see where each choice led."

"I would sure like that too, but since we can't, we can talk to the One who has all the answers. We'll pray and ask God to make it clear to both of us."

Olivia's lips thinned. She didn't reply.

Her dad came over and took Crystal and Olivia's hands in his hands as he glanced back and forth between them. "The decision is yours to make. I'd love for you to stay here and make the business yours, but I don't want to pressure either of you. Because number one, no matter what I desire, I want you both to follow what you believe God wants you to do. Whatever you decide, please don't allow fear to keep you from the adventure God has in store. My love for you both will never change no matter where you live."

Crystal swallowed hard to loosen her tightened throat. Even Olivia's lip was trembling.

"Thanks, Grandad." Olivia hugged him. Composing herself, she faced Katherine. "Are you sure you want my ideas on the first floor since I might not stay?"

"Regardless of what you decide," Katherine gave her a gentle smile. "I would very much appreciate your help."

Crystal stayed close to her dad. "If we do move here, I want you to be willing to accept payment, rent, or something to help offset your costs."

Her dad smiled in his gentle, soft way. "Don't worry about that. It will all work out."

# *Chapter 5*

Crystal breathed deeply of the new day scent of her beloved town. A light breeze cooled the air, lessening the humidity and rustling the changing leaves in Katherine's backyard.

Holding her coffee cup, Crystal sat beside her sister on the back deck. She glanced at Katherine. "Last night with the family was fun, but thinking about moving back to town without Mom and Uncle Kenneth being here is sad. I know it's been a few years, but I still miss them and the life we planned to have with them."

"It's hard to let go of a life we thought we would have. Death stinks for those of us left behind. We're left with memories and photos of our loved one's lives. I miss everything about Mom. I miss talking to her, her sweet hugs, and hearing her sing and play the piano. I miss watching Uncle Kenneth work at Knick Knacks or in his workshop. I miss seeing Sean's arm around you and watching him play with Olivia."

"Sean left imprints on my heart, sweet reminders that come when a song is played that he used to enjoy, a smell, a memory, or when something happens and I want to tell him about it. Even though it's been years, I miss so many things we did together. And I can't tell you how many times I wanted to call him to tell him something. I wish we could make phone calls to heaven."

"That would be nice." Katherine sighed and nodded. "Processing grief is different for each of us. Some stay busy to deal with the pain, and others can't, or don't want to, move forward. When a friend of mine lost her mom, she didn't show her outward grief. She just withdrew from everyone for about six months."

"I lost five pounds after Sean passed, probably from crying so much." Crystal's throat thick at the memories, she swiped a wayward tear off her cheek. "Olivia's still mad at God. It's been so long, but she's still angry."

"I'm sorry."

"One of mom's best advice she ever gave me when I married Sean was to make the most of our time together. She reminded me that not one of us knows how long we have. There are things I wish I had done differently, but her advice left me with fewer regrets. I always thought I would have the fairy tale life."

"You did, and you do," Katherine said. "Most fairy tales have a happy-ever-after, but the main character always goes through hard times."

Crystal narrowed her eyes at her sister. "Maybe I should have said I wanted an easy life."

"I think everyone will agree with you on that one. But it doesn't happen. Life is difficult, messy, and often heartbreaking."

"We should have been warned."

"Right." Katherine leaned toward her. "So when Olivia was born, would you have told her all the terrible things that would happen in her life?"

"Of course not." Crystal recoiled at that thought.

"Most of us want to know the future, but if we did, would any of us choose even to be born?"

"Probably not, but it would have been nice to have a written contract that said I'd have a good and very easy life."

"Okay. If you knew Sean would die young, would you have still married him?"

"Yes." Crystal didn't hesitate. "I wouldn't have missed a moment of our time together."

"There you go. I think God is very gracious not to tell us everything that will happen. God is in the past, present, and future. Whatever help we need, whatever comfort we need, whatever we go through, He will be with us to help us through. We're never promised an easy life, but in Christ, we are promised a wonderful happy-ever-after ending."

"Getting rather philosophical this morning, aren't you?"

Katherine grinned. "Are you impressed?"

"Maybe. You always had a good head on your shoulders."

"I don't know about that." Katherine looked away. "I've made some major mistakes."

"You? I didn't know about any mistakes."

"Well, do you think I would have broadcast my failures to the world?"

"I guess not." Curious to hear what she'd missed, Crystal leaned closer. "So, want to share?"

"Not really. Let's just say I didn't always live in a way that honored God or our family."

"I'm crushed." Crystal placed her hand on her chest as though she was having a heart attack.

"Oh, good grief. Did you really think I hadn't made mistakes?"

"I knew you weren't perfect, but I always looked up to you."

Katherine grinned as she sat straight in her chair. "I am five years older and two inches taller."

"You aren't going to tell me?"

Sighing, Katherine stared straight ahead, her gaze far away. "While I was in college, Mom and Dad flew out to see me. They told me they loved me and would always love me, but they disagreed with how I was living. They said I was welcome to return home, but not with my live-in-boyfriend. He could visit but never stay with me in their home."

Crystal couldn't stop her mouth from popping open. "You lived with a guy? Was it Michael?"

"No, it wasn't him." Katherine grimaced. "I'm not proud of what I did. After Mom and Dad talked to me, I was mad because I thought, how dare they be so judgmental. I was in college; I was smart and thought I knew what I was doing. It took a little while for me to come to my senses. My boyfriend was a handsome, fun-loving, party-going guy. I finally came to my senses and realized the relationship wasn't good, and I didn't want to live a life of partying, hangovers, guilt, and regrets. I was just wasting time by giving him pieces of me that didn't belong to him. So, I moved out and transferred to another university to finish my degree."

"I always wondered why you moved to that other school."

"Now you know. I would never have met Michael if I hadn't ended that other relationship. Mom and Dad were always gracious to me and even to that other boyfriend. Dad told me that loving someone means you want the best for them, and the best is always God's way, and God's way is the only way to find peace."

Crystal shook her head, trying to imagine all she'd missed. "I had no idea. I'm having to rewire my brain with all this new information. So, does Michael know about that other guy?"

"Yes, my sweet husband knows. I told him when we first started dating. He needed to know he wasn't getting a pure-as-snow woman."

"Well, I'm grateful you married Michael. He's a great guy, and now you have wonderful kids and grandkids. I think you made a very wise choice."

"Thanks. I had to step away from the things I knew so that I could venture into the unknown with God. I didn't know what was waiting for me, but God did. The best part is that when I returned to God, I found His grace had been waiting to welcome me home."

"See, I knew you had a good head on your shoulders."

"Not always, but I'm trying." Katherine's gaze settled on Crystal's face. "I know your heart hurts for Olivia. Keep loving her and keep praying for her. God didn't give up on me, and He won't give up on her."

Crystal nodded. "Thanks. I believe Olivia will find her way back to God. I just wish it was soon." She'd prayed so long for her daughter, and she would not stop praying.

A bird chirped in the tree branches, and a gentle breeze blew as they sat together in comfortable silence.

"So, do you think you will ever love again?" Katherine asked.

"I don't know. I didn't even consider dating those first years while Olivia was with me. Once she started dating Geoff, she moved into her apartment. And then, I did date a few guys. I had a heartbreak with one, and I didn't see others as a long-term relationship. No one comes close to Sean."

"Do you compare everyone to him?"

Crystal shrugged. "No, and yes. He was such a good guy and a great husband."

Katherine's grin turned mischievous. "You know Eric is a widower."

"We were just friends in high school."

"Just friends? You dated for a while, didn't you?"

Heat settled on Crystal's cheeks. "Yes, but we weren't serious or anything." Her leg started twitching as she thought of Eric's kind smile.

"Maybe you need to stop by and see how he's doing. Wouldn't it be nice to see your old friend?"

"I need to dance." Crystal sat down her coffee cup and rose to her feet.

"Oh, no." Katherine's eyes went wide. "You're still dancing?"

"Well, yes. Of course."

"It's not pretty, sis." Katherine grimaced. "Just not pretty at all. Your dance skill was probably tainted because mom taught music in our house when we were growing up."

"Why would that matter?"

"Because when the kids were practicing piano, they stopped and started. Maybe that's why your movements are herky-jerky."

"No, my dear sister. I am poetry in motion." Crystal waved her arms.

Katherine laughed. "More like haiku, no rhyme whatsoever."

"Rhythm and grace are highly overrated." Crystal opened her phone's music app and turned up the volume. "I am a swan fluidly, dramatically, beautifully moving to the music." She grabbed her sister's hands and yanked her to her feet. "Whatever your opinion, you need to get up and dance."

As the music played, they twirled and laughed until Katherine held up her hands. "Too much spinning." Face pale, she staggered to her chair. "I'm nauseous."

"Obviously, you need to dance more often." Ignoring the painful throbbing in her hip, Crystal made a dramatic curtsy.

"You know what, I think I do. And you need to take a leap of faith and get your tail back to Crawdad Beach. Let's get Olivia out of bed and get working on the building."

Looking over the items in the large canvas bag reserved for Katherine's deliveries, Eric addressed Sammie. "Is everything ready?"

The young man swiped his long brown bangs out of his eyes. "Yep, it's good to go. Want me to take it over to her?"

"Thanks. But, I've got it."

The door chimed, and Eric glanced up as it opened.

Chester, carrying a paper sack, came toward him. "Found a bunch of whatchamacallits during our last shopping outing for the antique store." He dropped the bag on the counter in front of him. "Found old nails, bolts, screws, hinges, and a few metal objects that I have no idea what they are. They are true whatchamacallits."

"Thanks." Eric grinned as he looked at the items. "You can put them in the bin. Someone might have use for them for something."

"I appreciate you keeping the tradition going," Chester emptied the contents into the big wooden box in the store since the early 1900s.

"It's a pleasure. Someone comes in about every week needing something strange for a project."

Chester leaned against the wooden shelves. "As a kid, I loved coming in and rummaging, looking to see what people had brought in."

"I did the same and must admit I still do." Eric pointed to the wall where the store displayed old farming utensils. "It's amazing to study the ingenuity of the early settlers."

"Doohickeys is a combination museum and hardware store. I think y'all have the best in the country."

"Thanks. I think so, too." Eric heaved the bag prepared for Katherine across his shoulder. "Thanks again for bringing in what you found. I need to deliver this across the street." He glanced over at Sammie. "Take care of everything. I'll be back soon."

Chester followed Eric out of the store and across the street. "You look like the hardware Santa with that big bag."

Eric grinned. "This Santa appreciates the business that Katherine brings to our store."

"Have you seen what she's doing this week?"

"No, I'm curious to check it out."

"I think you'll discover more than you expected." Chester gave him a mischievous smile. "I'll see you later." Whistling a happy tune, the man walked away.

Eric stepped inside the building and couldn't believe how much had been accomplished since the last time he'd seen it. Katherine and her crew must have been working overtime. Construction noises and the sounds of people talking came from upstairs and behind a door in the back. Not sure which way to go, he called out, "Hello!"

A brunette, petite woman stepped out from a door in the back.

Eric's jaw dropped at the sight of his beautiful friend. "Crystal?"

Wearing jeans and an oversized shirt that had probably once been white but now covered in dirt, Crystal smiled as she walked toward him. "Eric Reed, how are you?"

He dropped the bag he was carrying on the floor and gave her a quick hug. "I'm good. It's great to see you."

"You, too." She stepped out of his embrace and wiped off his shirt where she'd left a dirt stain. "Sorry about that. I'm helping Katherine get the building ready." Crystal brushed off her hair and clothes. "I must look pretty rough." She pointed at the door she had exited. "We've been doing demo work in the old loading dock."

"You might be a little dirty, but you're still pretty."

Her face took on a red tint. "Thanks. You look good, too.

Looking at her big brown eyes, Eric felt like a tongue-tied kid, unsure what to say. "I got a dog." He mentally face-palmed himself. Couldn't he have thought of something more intelligent to talk about?

Crystal smiled. "Good for you."

"It's just a puppy still, but it's cute." Good grief, he should just turn and walk away. He was a forty-five-year-old man. Rubbing his chin, he realized he should have shaved this morning. He probably looked pretty scruffy himself. Eric tried to look somewhat sophisticated. "So, how have you been?"

"Overall, okay." She shrugged as she smiled his way. "Life often takes unexpected turns."

"Yeah, it does." He studied her face, wondering what else might have happened in her life. "Are you in town for long?"

"Maybe. I'm not sure. I'm still praying about the next steps."

"You know, Crawdad Beach is a great place to live." Eric stepped closer to her. Even though she had obviously been working hard, she still smelled fresh, like she'd just gotten out of the shower. Even when she was younger, she always smelled good. He tried not to lean too close.

Crystal gazed up at him. "It is a great town. I have lots of happy memories here."

"I hope I'm some of them."

"We did have lots of fun, didn't we?" She leaned closer. "Did anyone figure out what we did on our late-night raids around town?"

"No." Eric shook his head. "No one ever discovered who planted flowers in the yards of the widows or who left groceries for people in need."

Crystal giggled. "I felt a little like Robin Hood when we did those things. Not that we stole from the rich or anything."

"No, but you used the money you made from waitressing at Tiddlywinks."

"You did, too. I mean not from waitressing, but from working with your dad at the store after school and on the weekends. It was worth it, wasn't it?"

"Oh, yeah. There are all kinds of legends around town about who did those things."

"So we're Crawdad Beach legends?"

Her smile made him temporarily breathless. "The best kind."

# *Chapter 6*

"You haven't stopped smiling."

At Katherine's comment, Crystal attempted a more neutral expression as she continued painting the trim around the apartment door. "Just thinking." She didn't want to share that her thoughts about Eric hadn't stopped since yesterday. Sure, she had seen him over the years when they came back for visits. He still had his sweet smile, and the hints of gray at his temples just made him look even more handsome.

"Those thoughts wouldn't have anything to do with the handsome, eligible, widowed bachelor named Eric, would they?"

"Why would you think that?" Crystal kept her voice nonchalant.

"Seriously? You two were all starry-eyed yesterday as you talked."

Crystal set her paintbrush down and looked at her sister. "I don't know what you're talking about."

Katherine laughed. "You both were so googly-eyed over one another you didn't even notice as I came down the stairs, picked up the bag Eric had brought, and took it upstairs with me."

"You did not!"

"Oh, yes. I did."

Crystal gulped as she thought about her conversation with Eric. "What did you hear?"

"Not much." Katherine's grin said more than her words. "Your secret is safe with me, you late-night raider, you."

Crystal stepped closer. "Promise you won't tell anyone."

"I won't, but it is nice to know my baby sister is one of the legendary Crawdadians. I always liked Eric and even like him more now that I know what you both did on your dates."

"We did have a blast."

"From the dreamy look on your face, I think it was more than just fun."

Heat rising up her back, Crystal turned back to painting. "Eric was always a nice guy." Although they had dated during high school, they had been good friends and had never gone too far with a physical relationship. How they kept things decent was beyond her, but it was nice to have the memories without any regrets. Since they both were single, could they pick up where they left off?

Crystal stopped her thoughts. She hadn't even decided she was moving to Crawdad Beach, and even though seeing Eric had been great, she didn't want to move here because of a possible relationship. How could she know what God wanted? She'd been praying and felt drawn back to her hometown, and everything seemed to be pointing that way, but emotions were too emotional. It was like if she didn't dance or have salsa, she'd get irritable. No, she couldn't trust her feelings.

Katherine nudged her. "Jeremiah thirty-three, three."

"What? Did you just tell me a Bible verse?"

"Yep, I could see your brain whirring away, looking for answers. Jeremiah thirty-three, three is the verse where God says call to Me, and I will answer you and show you great and mighty things you do not know. Other versions say unsearchable and hidden things, secrets. I know you're trying to decide whether or not to move. We would love to have you here, but we want you to make sure it's the right thing, the best thing, based on what God shows you."

Crystal nibbled on her bottom lip. "I've been praying for God's guidance."

"That's great," Katherine said. "There's also a verse in the Book of James that says if anyone lacks wisdom, they should ask God. So, be specific in your requests so that you will know when God specifically answers. Maybe also request a Bible verse or verses to confirm that you hear the answer correctly."

"Okay, I guess I should be more direct in my prayers than just praying *help, please*."

Katherine chuckled. "I do that quite often. The family is praying God will make it clear to you and Olivia. For now, I'm glad you're here. I've missed you."

"Thanks, I've missed you too." It was so good to be back in Crawdad Beach, but was it right for her to move here? Continuing to paint, she silently prayed, asking God to confirm with either yes or no and Bible verses. A few verses from her daily Bible reading about thornbushes, myrtles, and cypress trees came to mind. Why would she think that? She set down her paintbrush and addressed her sister. "Give me a minute, okay? I'm going to go to the other room. I'll be back."

"Sure. Take whatever time you need."

Crystal closed the door behind her and opened her phone's Bible software app to find the verses. She searched for the words about the plants. Stopping at chapter fifty-five in Isaiah, chill bumps popped on her arm as she read verses about going out with joy and being led with peace by God, and it went on to say that instead of the thorn bush, the cypress would come up, and instead of briars, the myrtle would come up. Was that her answer? Back in Texas, she had thorns and briars coming up from the untended yard next to hers, whereas Crawdad Beach had beautiful crepe myrtles and cypress trees by the river. She continued praying, and an incredible peace came over her. Sinking to her knees, she prayed and thanked God for the answer.

Excited and grateful, she left the room and returned to her sister. "I made a direct request to God, and I believe I got a direct answer."

"You did?" Katherine gave her a hopeful look.

"I'm moving here."

Katherine squealed and hugged her tight. "I'm so excited!"

"I am, too." They held each other and jumped up and down like little girls. Crystal's stomach dropped as she considered what else her moving might mean. "But what about Olivia?"

Katherine's eyes gentled. "God has a plan for her, too. When God calls us to step out in faith, we need to trust Him with our lives and those we love."

"Well, I'm excited and a little scared. I so want my baby girl with me."

"Your baby girl is a big girl, and God is a big God."

"Mom! Could you come down here for a minute?"

Crystal jerked her attention at the sound of Olivia's voice.

Katherine nodded toward Crystal. "Sounds like trouble."

Hurrying down the steps, Crystal stopped in front of her daughter. "What's wrong?"

Olivia jammed her phone in the back pocket of her jeans. "This is not the life I thought I would have—not by a long shot. No matter what I pray for, God blocks my path." She paced back and forth, not even looking at

Crystal. "First, I lose my dad, and now Geoff. He should have asked me to marry him, not do this." She mumbled what sounded like a string of curse words. "I'll probably get zapped by a lightning bolt. Why does God hate me? It's not like I asked for much. I wanted Dad to live, to be with me, but he's gone."

Olivia's gaze flicked to Crystal. "I'd been a good girl, at least for most of my life. I went to church and was a nice daughter, but still, Dad died. God turned a deaf ear to my many prayers. And now, Geoff pushed me out of his life. How could he do that to me?"

Crystal laid a hand on her daughter's arm. "What's happened?"

Olivia blinked back the moisture gathering in her eyes. "Geoff called, and he's already replaced me."

"*What?* Replaced you? You mean at the restaurant? You haven't even given notice. Had you?"

"No! What a jerk! I hadn't even decided what I was going to do."

"That's not right. How can Geoff do that?"

Olivia crossed her arms over her chest. "He hired one of the women who was on the show with him. The big-chested blonde he flirted with the most."

Crystal put her hand over her mouth for a moment. "I am so sorry. Wait a minute. One of the reasons the restaurant received such high ratings is because of the desserts and pastries you created."

"I know. It just stinks." Olivia growled. "I didn't want to return to the restaurant, but I wanted to leave on my own terms. Instead, Geoff said he would make me the new woman's assistant."

Crystal sucked in a breath. "I'm not thinking nice thoughts about him."

"Me neither. I can't believe this. I mean, I've seen the signs of what Geoff was like for a long time. I guess I just didn't want to deal with it or believe it." Olivia shoved a wayward hair behind her ear. "I thought I loved him, and he loved me, but I was just kidding myself."

"I'm sorry, honey."

Olivia lasered a look her way. "You never liked Geoff."

"No, I didn't, but I'm still sorry for your pain."

Olivia crossed to the front window and stared outside. "Why can't things be different? I've worked for years at the restaurant and dated Geoff for years. Now, they've both been taken from me. It isn't fair."

Crystal stood next to her. "I'm sorry about what Geoff did."

"Yeah, well. I'm not surprised. I'm hurt, angry, mad, disappointed, and tired of the relationship."

"You know, if you move here, you could tell Geoff you're leaving Houston to run your own business."

"I can think of lots of things I'd like to tell him. None of which *you* would approve." Olivia shook her head, then gazed at Crystal. "It would be nice to rub in his face that I owned my own business. He might be the chef, but he's not the owner."

"So, would you be open to moving here?" Crystal tried not to sound too much like she was begging, but she was. "This would be a fresh start. I'll help you, and your family is here to help."

"I don't know. I've never lived anywhere else." Olivia rubbed the back of her neck. "I don't want to return to the restaurant with Geoff, and I will *never* be his new girlfriend's assistant." Olivia fisted her hands and looked like she really wanted to hit something. "How could I have been so stupid? And why did I want to hold on to Geoff? He was an egotistical narcissist." Olivia turned to her. "Let's go for it. I don't want to have anything to do with Geoff."

Crystal felt like shouting hallelujah and start dancing but instead toned her reaction to a pleasant smile. "I'll call the realtor and accept the offer for the house sale, and we'll get back to Houston to get everything ready to move that we want to bring with us. The apartment upstairs can be our home base for now. And if any furniture doesn't fit, we can leave it in the garage or with family members."

Olivia shook her head. "I don't have much worth moving. Most of my time was at work or with Geoff." Olivia swallowed hard. "I'll donate most of my belongings so someone else can use them. I'm ready for a new start."

Crystal sent a silent thank you to God. "I'm thrilled, and I know the family will be too. So, are you ready to be the owner of whatever you want to make this?" She waved her hand around.

"Me?" Olivia tilted her head. "I thought you would be the owner, and I'd be the helper."

"Nope. You are the extraordinary pastry chef, and this business is all yours. So think about what you want to call it, and let's tell Katherine, and I'll call my dad." Crystal squeezed Olivia in a bear hug. "The adventure begins."

Nearing closing time, Eric came out of his office and noticed Henry standing at the screws, nuts, and bolt section.

"Can I help you find anything?" Eric walked over to the kind man.

Henry held up an old rusty, flat-head screw. "I need to replace these. We need six."

"Interior or exterior?"

"Interior, please," Henry said. "Jeremy, Chester, and I are restoring old tables to use in the building Katherine's turning into a bakery."

"It makes my mouth water just thinking about a bakery. So, who's the new owner?" Eric tried not to show how hopeful he was about the possibility that it would be Crystal.

"My granddaughter Olivia is a pastry chef, so she'll run the business, and Crystal will help."

"They're staying?" Eric stopped himself from pumping a celebratory fist in the air. He'd been praying hard, more like begging God, to get Crystal back in town.

"Yes, we're grateful, as I'm sure you are, that they're moving here." Henry's smile revealed that he knew some of Eric's thoughts.

"Well, let me know if I can do anything." Eric handed Henry a package of screws for his project.

"I think we have the table situation under control. Crystal and Olivia will leave in a few days and then return in a few weeks to stay for good." Henry's smile looked relieved, grateful, and excited. "Perhaps you can join us for a welcome to Crawdad Beach party when they return to town."

"I would be honored. Just let me know the day, time, and what I can bring."

"I'll keep you updated." Henry smiled, paid for his purchase, and left.

Eric made a mental list of things he needed to take care of in the next few weeks. He'd put off his house projects for too long. He needed to ensure his house looked good if Crystal ever came over. Maybe he was thinking too far ahead, but he hoped they could pick up their relationship. Then again, what if they did start dating again? What would it be like now that he and Crystal were adults and had adult children? And what would his daughters think?

Last time they were home, they'd asked him if he would ever seriously date anyone, and they even seemed open to the idea. Not that anyone could ever replace their mom, but they seemed eager for him to have his own life. Maybe it was because they both had serious boyfriends. The girls lived together and were best friends. His oldest was finishing her Master's degree, and his youngest would receive a Bachelor's degree in the spring.

He and his daughters loved their mom; nothing about that would change. They would never, ever forget Amy. Some of his distant relatives would be shocked that Eric was even considering dating again. They seemed to want him to grieve forever.

Eric redirected his thoughts. Maybe nothing would come from Crystal moving back to town, but he still needed to get his house ready. It wasn't messy; he'd just put off any deep cleaning. Once Crystal moved to town, maybe she would be willing to at least have dinner with him at Tiddlywinks and come to his place for dessert.

He would enjoy her friendship and be very open if things progressed beyond just friends.

# *Chapter 7*

She still believed leaving Texas was right, but leaving the home where she and Sean had raised their daughter was more challenging than she had imagined. Crystal kept her focus on the road. Her house sale had been completed, and all their belongings were on a moving truck from Houston. She'd fought tears on and off as they drove away from where she'd lived for over twenty years. Olivia didn't cry; she just looked resigned.

Fortunately, the closer they got to Crawdad Beach, the more Crystal's grief lifted and the more excited she was about moving to South Carolina. Even Olivia seemed more relaxed and upbeat. During the drive, they planned what the business would look like and even tried to devise a catchy name. They hadn't decided on anything yet but had laughed at some of their goofy ideas.

Finally, in town, Crystal turned her car past Crawdad Beach's Main Street and slowly drove past stately, distinguished houses, two-story Victorians, a red-brick colonial house with white columns, and smaller older homes.

She stopped in front of David and Marie's craftsman-type house, where her dad lived in his private quarters.

Olivia yawned and stretched. "I'm ready to be able to stand up and walk around."

"I am, too. We've traveled over 1100 miles." Crystal rubbed her sore hip as she stepped out of the car and stretched her back. "After dinner, we'll stay at Katherine's place until the apartment is ready and our furniture arrives."

"Sounds good." Olivia walked next to her as they walked up the sidewalk. "The shipping company said my car should be here the day after tomorrow. Speaking of cars, how many people will be here for dinner?"

Crystal looked around as they approached the front door. "Dad said the family wanted to welcome us to town, but from all the vehicles, it looks like most of Crawdad Beach is here."

Sounds of talking and laughter came from the house. Crystal rang the doorbell and stepped inside. A huge welcome sign hung across the opening leading to the family room. Her dad and what looked like half of Crawdad Beach started shouting *Welcome Home*!

Her dad gave them big hugs while his little dog, Filbert, danced around them, wagging like crazy.

Crystal smiled as she looked at the familiar faces of her sister, Katherine, and her husband, Michael, their son David, his wife Marie, their twins, and their little dog, Filbertina. Crystal's niece Tess was there with her husband Paul and their twins. Aunt Helen had brought her great-nephew, Jeremy, and his new wife, Grace. Even their lifelong family friends Chester and his wife Maybelline and her ever-present bouffant hairdo were there.

As glad as she was to see friends and family, Crystal's heart did a happy dance in her chest when she spotted Eric. Wearing jeans and a blue shirt that brought out the blue in his eyes, he patiently waited as her family hugged and welcomed her home.

He stepped toward her. "You're dad invited me. I'm glad you're back. You've been gone too long. I've missed you." He gave her a polite, one-armed hug.

Even at the casual embrace, she felt her cheeks heat. "Thanks. It's good to be back in town."

The evening passed in a fun blur as she ate the best homemade meal she'd had in ages. Her family definitely had great cooks. After clearing the table and cleaning the kitchen, part of the group settled around the dining table, and the rest moved to the family room.

Her friends and relatives talked and laughed as the kids played with the dogs. Her dad stood beside Chester as he told a funny story, and Olivia laughed with her cousins.

Eric sat next to Crystal on the couch. "You glad to be here?"

"Yes, very much so."

"Was it hard to leave Texas?"

"Yes." Crystal nodded as old memories returned. "It wasn't easy. I don't have any doubts about coming here, but it's hard to leave behind so many memories, you know?"

His eyes held compassion. "I can't imagine. I've lived here all my life."

"You have any regrets about never going anywhere else?"

"No. I think I'm a lifelong Crawdadian." He held up his hands and tapped his fingers together like a crawdad. "I'm grateful to have been born and raised here."

"You look pretty good for a Crawdad man."

Smiling, he tilted his head. "You used to tell me that when we were dating."

A flurry of fun and sweet memories passed through her mind as warmth settled on her cheeks. "We did have some good times, didn't we?"

He grinned. "Yep. You still dancing?"

"Yes, much to my family's chagrin."

"You're a great dancer."

Crystal scoffed. "Right, says the man with two left feet and no rhythm."

Eric nudged her shoulder. "We made a good pair as we danced."

"More like herky-jerky people in our valiant but woefully inadequate attempts."

He laughed. "We might not have done it right, but nobody had more fun than we did." He puffed out his chest. "We won an award, remember? We were voted most likely *never* to win a dance contest."

Crystal giggled at the memories of their friends watching them with their horrified expressions. She smiled at her sweet, handsome friend. "Eric, thank you for all the fun we had."

He leaned close to her ear. "We had a great time, and I remember some great kissing."

She swallowed hard as heat enveloped her body. "Maybe we should dance." She grabbed her phone, turned on her music app, and found their favorite dance song. "Let's have some fun."

As the music started, Eric jumped up and moved the coffee table out of the way.

They danced, and even though she remembered the steps, Crystal still couldn't get them right. Eric didn't seem to care; his arms flailed as his body moved in time with her, which wasn't necessarily to the music.

The younger members of her family joined them while Chester and Maybelline danced more of a waltz. Her dad clapped along with the music. The little twins giggled and twirled. Olivia joined in since she obviously knew the correct dance moves. Even the dogs were jumping and running around.

The music ended, and her family and friends clapped for one another as though they had all been in a Broadway show.

Laughing, Crystal and Eric took a bow together.

After the most fun she'd had in ages, Crystal ignored her throbbing hip and collapsed on the couch next to Eric.

Eric wiggled his eyebrows. "You still got the moves."

"Thanks, I can say that without shame. I might not be in time with the music, but I've got moves. We make a good team."

"You bet we do. No one else could look as out of step yet in sync as we do."

Crystal giggled and sighed. How grateful she was to be back home.

"Hey, Eric," Chester called out as he walked toward them. "Let me show you a picture of something I found at an estate sale the other day." He pointed his phone at Eric. "Any idea what this is? It looks like a torture tool to me."

Eric squinted as he studied the picture. "I have no clue. It's definitely a whatchamacallit."

"Maybe it's one of those things knights used when they were fighting," Chester moved his arm in a chopping motion.

Olivia walked over, glanced at the photo, then laughed. "You two are too funny. That's an old meat tenderizer."

"You mean like a meat mallet?" Chester asked. "I know what those things are. Maybelline has one, but this thing looks more deadly than that."

Olivia grinned. "The only reason I know is because I saw one like it on a food blog the other day. It's an ancient version. Did you find anything else like this?"

"Yep," Chester said. "I've got them in a box in my garage. Maybelline and I were going to take them to Jeremy and see if he wanted to sell them at Knick Knacks."

Olivia waved over Jeremy. "Hey, would you mind if I checked out what Chester has before you see them?"

Jeremy smiled. "No problem at all. I know you're looking for items for your new business."

"Thanks. I appreciate it." Olivia turned back to Chester. "Could I come to see them tomorrow? Old cooking utensils would look cool on an accent wall in the bakery."

"Sure. Drop by anytime. I was planning on working in the yard in the morning anyway." Chester motioned to Crystal's dad. "Henry, did you tell them what we've been working on?"

"Not yet." Her dad joined them. "Looks like now might be a good time. Chester, Jeremy, and I have been working on tables for your business."

Chester scrolled through the photos on his phone and held it toward Olivia. "Check these out."

"Wow, those are great. They will be perfect." Olivia hugged her grandad and thanked Chester and Jeremy.

Thankful to see Olivia enjoying herself, Crystal stood to see what they were talking about. "Where did you find all those old bistro tables and chairs?"

"All over the place," Chester said. "We've been working on them since Katherine started the renovations."

Her dad nodded. "We've already put most of them in the building." He turned to Olivia. "You can choose the ones you want to keep, and Jeremy will sell the rest at Knick Knacks."

Olivia's lip trembled. "I can't believe how nice you're all being." She hugged her grandad again and then ran off to tell her cousins.

A little emotional, Crystal thanked the men and settled on the couch beside Eric.

Eric grinned at her. "They've been working hard to prepare things for you and Olivia. With your family and friends around, I don't think you have anything to worry about."

"It's exciting and a little scary stepping into uncharted territory."

He leaned closer. "That's where the best adventures are found." Eric's grin faltered as his eyebrows drew together. "You're rubbing your hip again. Is it hurting?"

Crystal shifted and put her hands in her lap. She hadn't even been aware of what she was doing. "It's nothing. Probably just a sore muscle or something."

"You should check it out. There's a good orthopedic group closer to the beach. Most of the people in town use them." He took out his phone and texted her the number. "Give them a call. I can tell it's bothering you more than you admit. I've noticed you limping and rubbing that hip several times."

"You have? Well, don't worry. It's probably from doing so much working with Katherine, packing, moving, driving for hours, and dancing. It's probably nothing."

"Promise me you'll check."

Crystal sighed. "Fine. I'll call soon." She turned away and pretended to pay attention to the other conversations in the room. There was no time to worry about her aching hip; she had too much to do to ensure she and Olivia settled in Crawdad Beach. Maybe she could wait a few months, and it would disappear.

Sensing Eric was still staring at her, Crystal rose to her feet and walked to the kitchen to find a quiet place away from the family where she could rub her hip without anyone noticing. She opened the walk-in pantry door and stepped inside. Biting her lip, she tried not to whimper at the stabbing pain in her hip. What on earth had she done to make her body so mad at her?

"Crystal." His voice quiet; Eric stepped next to her and leaned close. "I'm not trying to push or pry, but please promise me you will get checked out with a doctor."

She gave an exasperated sigh. "Fine. I promise."

"Thank you." He lifted her chin. His eyes were tender. "Now that my dance partner is back in town, I need you healthy."

"You only care because of my beautifully coordinated dance moves."

Eric brushed a hand against her cheek. "Not only that. I care about your beautiful heart."

Her vision blurred at his kindness and gentleness. Before she let tears fall, she hugged him tight. "Thank you, Eric."

He enveloped her in a gentle embrace and rested his head on hers. "I'm glad you're home, Crystal."

Enjoying his clean scent and the feel of his strong arms around her, she snuggled against him. "Me too."

After the party ended, Crystal and Olivia drove to Katherine's house. Even though it had been two hours since she and Eric had hugged and talked, Crystal still felt like her feet weren't touching the ground. She finished brushing her teeth and entered the spare bedroom she shared with Olivia.

Olivia, already in pajamas in one of the twin beds, looked up with a serious expression. "Tonight was a blast, but I need to talk to you about something." She leveled her gaze on her. "Let me see if I understand about Eric. You're both from a small town, are long-lost loves who dated in high school, have both lost spouses, and you will be involved in running a bakery. Please tell me he does *not* wear flannel shirts."

Crystal sat on the twin bed she would be using and gave her daughter a curious look. "I'm not sure. What would that matter?"

"Because it seems like this is one of those syrupy sweet movies you see on television."

Crystal chuckled. "Oh, my goodness. You're right. It does."

Olivia studied her for a moment. "So, how well do you like Eric?"

"He's a very nice guy. He was sweet in high school and still very sweet."

"Sweet or not, just don't jump into something too quick."

Crystal almost laughed at Olivia's serious expression. "I won't. Eric is my friend. But, would you be upset if it turned into something more than friends?"

"No. Not at all. Dad has been gone for over seven years. I'm surprised you haven't already met someone else. It was nice to watch you having so much fun tonight, even though it's incredibly disturbing that neither you nor Eric has any rhythm. I would have recorded you on my phone, but it would have gone viral, and the shame would have been on our family forever."

Crystal giggled at her daughter's mock disgust. "It was so much fun. My stomach still hurts from laughing."

"Mine too. I am glad we're here." Olivia's smile dimmed, and her gaze dropped to the floor. "I haven't heard a peep from Geoff, but I did hear from a friend who works at the restaurant. Geoff moved in with the woman he hired. Plus, I found out most of the other contestants in the cooking competition didn't stay the whole time. They were free to fly home on the weekends. Evidently, Geoff was staying the whole time with that woman."

"Ouch. I am so sorry."

"Don't be." Olivia shrugged a shoulder. "It stinks, but it shows me even more that it was time to leave Texas and move on."

"Well, now you don't have to worry about him anymore. With the new business, you are your own boss and free to create pastries to your heart's content."

"I am looking forward to that. Tess and Marie said they could help when their kids are at school. And, Maybelline and Chester, and Aunt Helen said they also wanted to help."

Crystal grinned as she imagined them huddled together, following Olivia's instructions. "Working with you and family members and friends will be fun."

"I know, right? I'm not sure how busy we will be and what will need to be done until we move forward. We still need computer software with a point-of-sale system to check out the customers, and I also need to apply for and get a bunch of different business licenses. I'm ready to get started. I still can't believe Granddad is giving us the building and the business. But, once we get things going, I want to pay him back."

"Paying Grandad back will be great, but there's no rush. He wants you to have time to succeed." Even though her dad had generously made a way for Olivia to open the business, Crystal still couldn't wrap her head around all they'd need to open a bakery and make it profitable in their little town. While in the hotel business, she worked the front desk, the dining area, and management. Now, she hoped and prayed she'd be a help to her daughter.

"Granddad wants both of us to succeed, right?"

Crystal nodded. "Right. Both of us. I'm here to help in whatever way you need me."

"I can't wait to try some of my ideas. Thank goodness I didn't leave my best recipes with Geoff."

"I'm sure our family will be happy to be taste testers. Once everything is ready, we can have a private opening."

A sly smile crossed Olivia's face. "I imagine Eric might be stopping by often, too."

Crystal didn't hide her smile at that thought. She fluffed her pillow and laid down on her bed. "Well, we have a busy day ahead. We better get to sleep." After turning off the light, she smiled as she stared at the ceiling. Tonight with family was great, and the time with Eric made it even more wonderful. Eric's words ran through her mind and cuddled her heart. *I'm glad you're home.*

She cuddled close to her pillow. Tomorrow morning they would continue to help Katherine and her crew finish the building. Her hip throbbed at the thought. She tried to adjust, and still, the pain continued. The last thing she needed was anything that might burden Olivia or her family.

Crystal rolled over, closed her eyes, and prayed God would take away her hip pain and let her get on with her new life.

# *Chapter 8*

The following day, Crystal had to force her mouth close as she surveyed the building's downstairs kitchen. How did so much get finished and installed since they'd been gone? Huge ovens, an industrial gas range, mixers, microwaves, freezers and refrigerators, food prep surfaces and equipment, pots, pans, mixing bowls, food processors, blenders, mixers, storage containers and shelving, a big sink, dishwashing sink, dishwasher, along with a myriad of other supplies.

Olivia's smile was the biggest Crystal had seen in years. "Aunt Katherine, you did good! I love what you found."

Crystal glanced at Katherine. "I can't believe all you have in here. Everything looks expensive."

"They would have been," Katherine said, "but we got a great deal on used equipment from a bakery that closed in Charlotte. The owner had retired and was ready to move closer to where her children live. We practically bought everything she had."

"It's awesome," Olivia said as she walked around the kitchen. "I told Aunt Katherine what would be needed, and her electrician went with her to ensure everything looked good before they made the purchase."

"I wouldn't know what to do with most of them." Crystal stood next to a colossal commercial mixer. "This probably has a bigger engine than my first car. Whatever happened to the days of mixing bowls, rolling pins, and flour sifters?"

Olivia chuckled. "Without commercial equipment, feeding more than a big family would be difficult. Last night, I talked to David and Uncle Michael, and they said they could order flour, sugar, and most of the basic supplies. It's nice to have family members who own and manage the grocery store."

"I'm sure they'll give you a great deal." Crystal grinned at the thought. "And remember that Mr. and Mrs. Hollis promised they would help if you needed additional information about running a business in Crawdad Beach."

"Howdy, family!" Crystal's niece, Tess, carrying a large canvas bag, entered the kitchen. "I'm here to paint."

Olivia squealed and ran to her cousin. "I'm so excited." Olivia turned back toward them. "Guess what? I thought of a name for the bakery last night. I called and hired Tess to paint a mural on the wall next to the checkout counter of a cute cartoon crawdad wearing an apron and holding a rolling pin in one of his claws and an oven mitt in the other. And the name is..." Olivia paused and was practically dancing in excitement. "Rolling in the Dough."

"I love that!" Crystal and Katherine said together.

Olivia grinned. "Well, since I didn't want to use our last name because Baker's Bakery wouldn't be too exciting and a Parisian name didn't fit in a town that has businesses with the name of Doohickeys, Tiddlywinks, Knick Knacks, and Curl and Dye, and has a cartoon crawdad as a mascot. I knew I needed something that blended in with the playfulness of our city."

"You are wise, little one." Crystal hugged her daughter. "I love the name and the idea for the mural." She turned to her niece. "Tess, you've done such a wonderful job with all the murals around town."

"Thanks, Aunt Crystal. It's been a fun little side hobby."

Olivia grabbed Tess's arm. "Come on, and I'll show you where I want you to paint." The two ran out of the room.

Crystal moved closer to Katherine. "I can't thank you and Dad enough for all you are doing for us."

"It's our pleasure. We're grateful you two are here with us."

"We are, too. It's great to see Olivia excited again. I don't think she realized how much stress she was under working at that restaurant. I know she enjoyed her work, but the hours were long, and I don't think she ever received the credit she deserved for all she did to make them successful. Plus, I'm grateful she is away from Geoff."

"It is good to see her excited, and I agree about her ex-boyfriend. At least I hope he is an ex and stays that way."

Crystal nodded. "I hope so, too."

"Fire!" Wide-eyed, Olivia barged into the kitchen and waved her hand toward the front door. "Did you hear me? Fire! There's smoke coming out of one of the loft apartment windows."

Crystal started to run, but Katherine stopped her as she glanced out the window. "No reason to worry. Looks like Marcus was trying to cook again."

"Well, hurry and check." Olivia pushed Crystal, Katherine, and Tess to the sidewalk out front.

A nice-looking, dark-haired young man wearing glasses stood coughing on his balcony across the street. Glancing at them, he held up his hands. "Sorry! I forgot about my meal on the stove again."

Katherine chuckled. "I probably should charge him extra for his apartment rental. Marcus gets so immersed in his work he forgets what he's doing. Plus, he has absolutely no cooking skills. How many people do you know that burn ramen noodles? It's a good thing I put a sprinkler system in the apartments. Thankfully, we haven't needed them yet, but his apartment's smoke alarm should get hazard pay."

Tess went back to painting, and Crystal followed Katherine to the kitchen.

Wondering where Olivia had gone, Crystal spotted her daughter across the street talking to the young man. "Well, that's interesting. Olivia may have discovered another reason to enjoy living in Crawdad Beach."

"Marcus is a nice guy," Katherine said. "He's Alexa's brother and a software security specialist working for Dustin Bowman's firm. Dad and Chester checked him out because they were worried he was interested in Grace when he first moved here."

"Okay, let me try to remember." Crystal tapped a finger against her chin. "Dustin is the mayor and also runs the software security firm. Marcus's sister Alexa is the young woman with a lightning bolt shaved in her hair. And, Alexa and Grace were roommates before Alexa married Tony, and Grace married Jeremy."

"Good job." Katherine gave her a thumbs up. "I'm impressed you remembered."

"Thank goodness Dad kept me updated on what was happening in town."

"Lots going on here in Crawdad Beach. The CBPT is grateful Jeremy and Grace got together."

"CBPT?" Crystal asked.

"You know, the Crawdad Beach Prayer Team," Katherine grinned. "You won't find a sweeter group of people. They don't gossip or have an agenda other than God's best for the person they pray for. They don't just pray for God's will. They pray for God's perfect will to be done."

"That sounds wonderful. I hope the prayer group is praying for me."

"Dad is on that team, so I can guarantee everyone in our family has been, or is currently, on their prayer list. Dad's even been in here praying over the building."

Crystal sighed. "Just thinking about that, I feel better already." Her dad was the best. It was a shame everyone couldn't have a father like hers. Thankfully, everyone had the opportunity to be fathered by their good, loving Heavenly Father.

Olivia came into the kitchen, followed by Chester. "Look who I found."

"Hey, you two. Do you need any help today?" Chester asked.

Katherine nodded. "Sure, we'll take you up on that offer."

Chester grabbed a screwdriver and pointed it toward them. "Did you know this building was used for criminal purposes in the 1930s?"

"What?" Katherine said. "I didn't know anything about this. I thought it had been a clothing store and then a small department store."

"According to the Crawdad historians," Chester said, "the building was first a clothing store, and when it closed in 1936, it stood empty for a year. The Bonnie brothers, who were not nice guys, bought it for practically nothing. They boarded up the front windows, didn't talk to anyone, and went into the building in the morning and left late at night. Everyone in town wondered what they were up to, and several old-timers even set their chairs up across the street to watch."

Chester's expression, serious but mischievous, leaned closer. "One night, when all the stores on Main Street were closed, a boom shook the town. People ran to see what happened. Dust and super-smelly debris filled the air, and a huge hole was next to the bank. Screams and desperate yells came from the crater. As the townspeople crept forward, they found the Bonnie brothers covered in sewage, trying to claw their way out of the nasty, slimy hole. The brothers thought they had tunneled to the bank and dynamited the vault, but instead, they had blasted open a concrete sewage tank."

"Oh, no! Ack!" Shuddering, Crystal joined in laughing with the others. "Why didn't we know about this? We grew up here?"

Still grinning, Chester clicked his tongue in mock disproval. "You must not have been listening when your elders were sharing their stories."

"Obviously, I need to pay more attention." Crystal glanced at Olivia. "Speaking of paying attention, what did you think of Marcus?"

Olivia's cheeks tinted pink. "I went over to chew him out for almost burning down Aunt Katherine's apartment building. But then. Well, he's nice. Handsome. Smart. Has a good sense of humor." She shrugged. "Not that I was paying attention or anything."

Chester's eyebrows raised. "You met Marcus? He's a good guy."

Crystal gave him a sly smile. "I heard you and Dad checked him out."

"We did. Not ashamed of that fact. Henry and I just wanted to make sure he was an okay young man."

Olivia gave him an inquisitive look. "So, do you and Granddad check out everyone who moves to town?"

Chester's gaze lifted to the ceiling. "I will neither confirm nor deny that question."

Pointing to his available rakes, Eric stood beside the young blonde-haired woman shopping in his store. "This is a twenty-four-inch, double-tinted leaf rake with a detachable eight-inch hand rake that helps get to those hard-to-reach places. I have one myself. I detach the small one and use it almost like an extra hand. "

"That sounds great," the woman said. "I'll take it. My daughter will probably think the small rake is for her."

Eric smiled as he walked her to the counter. "Start them out young while they still enjoy helping." He pointed to his employee. "Sammie will help you check out. Thanks for shopping at Doohickeys."

Hoping Katherine needed something from the store, Eric returned to his office to check his email since she sometimes would text, email, call, or run over to pick up any needed supplies. He hadn't heard from her for a few days and hoped to have an excuse to see Crystal. Besides wanting to see her, he wanted to check on how her hip was doing and make sure she had an appointment with a doctor.

He glanced at the photo of his family taken a few years before his wife had passed. When Amy started feeling bad, she had put off going to the doctor. He just about had to drag her to get checked. By the time she'd been diagnosed with Leukemia, it was too late for most of the treatments that would have been available if they had caught it sooner.

Eric squeezed the muscle tightening in his neck. What if something was wrong with Crystal? How could he ever go through the pain of losing someone else he cared about? And would he even consider traveling down that road again?

# Chapter 9

Surveying the mountain of boxes waiting to be unpacked, Crystal took a drink of sweet, iced tea as she leaned against the kitchen counter. Their little apartment hummed with activity as family members, along with Eric, helped get them settled. Olivia stayed downstairs to check off the moving list as their belongings were removed from the truck and carried into the building. Since her daughter would be the business owner, Crystal gave her the master suite. She wanted her daughter to know the business, and that the apartment belonged mainly to her.

Eric placed his tool belt on the counter and stood next to Crystal. "I finished hanging all the window blinds for you."

"Thank you for doing that for us." Crystal glanced around, trying to remember where she had left her purse. "How much do I owe you?"

He held up his hand. "No charge. It's my welcome to Crawdad Beach gift. The hardware store owner gave me a discount on the products. Actually, it's an advertising ploy. I can point to your windows from the street and show customers what the blinds look like from the other side."

Crystal smiled at his cute grin. "Well, whatever the reason, it's very sweet of you. Thank you." She handed him a bottle of water and took a long drink of tea to try to cool her urge to step into his arms for another hug.

Eric took a swig of water and wiped his mouth with the back of his hand. "The movers have just about finished. Didn't take them long at all."

"It's a good thing I had a big garage sale, and Olivia sold and gave away most of her belongings. When you have to pay the movers by the pound, it's easier to get rid of things."

"Well, just remember, Doohickeys will give you a great deal on any items you might need for your new home." His gaze dropped to her lips, then quickly back to her eyes as his neck reddened. "The owner is very generous with pretty brunettes."

Crystal grinned. "That would be very kind of that owner. I hear he's a good guy."

"It's a good thing I'm a native Crawdadian, or your dad, and Chester would be running a background check on me."

"I'm sure you would pass with flying colors."

Eric shrugged. "I hate to admit it, but I've had a pretty boring existence. I don't even have a college degree."

"Why would that matter? You run a very successful business. I know some people who spent so much on their education that they'll have difficulty getting out of debt. Others have degrees and work at jobs that don't even require one. Besides that, you've always been smart. I think it's wonderful that you've lived here all your life."

"Thanks. I did take a few business and accounting courses at the community college. Dad needed me to keep working in the store. Honestly, I didn't want to go anywhere else. Unfortunately, my girls might not feel the same way since they're both in serious relationships with guys who live in another state."

"They have long-distance relationships?"

Eric shook his head. "No, they're in college in North Carolina. I expect to get phone calls any day with the happy news of engagements. Fortunately, I like both the young men they're dating. I just wish they would bring my girls back here to live. I'm hoping they'll at least settle within driving distance."

"Will they be coming home for Thanksgiving or Christmas?"

"Yep. I think the girls are more excited about seeing my new dog than seeing me."

"I'm sure that's not true," Crystal said.

"Well, you haven't met Gadget. She's an adorable, loving little pup."

From various parts of the apartment, phones began signaling text messages.

Eric took his phone out of his back pocket and read a message. "Oh, no. Lucy has fallen and is on her way to the hospital."

Crystal grimaced. "Lawnmower Lucy?"

"Yes, her son is with her and asked for prayer. I hate that for Lucy. We need to pray she'll be able to return home."

Work around the apartment stopped as others seemed to be in prayer.

Eric took Crystal's hand in his. "Want to pray with me?"

She nodded and closed her eyes. Eric's sweet prayer for Lucy brought tears to Crystal's eyes. Sean never prayed out loud. Praying had been a private matter for him.

Finished with his prayer, Eric squeezed her hand. "Better get back to work. I'm sure you want as much done as possible before tonight." He took a few steps, then turned back to her. "It sure is nice to know you're back in town for good."

Heat settled on Crystal's cheeks. "It's really nice to be home."

"Mom!" Olivia's excited voice came from downstairs.

"Better go see what she needs." Crystal hurried to her daughter as Eric followed behind.

With a huge smile, Olivia stood beside an old bicycle with a frayed wicker basket. "Look what Jeremy brought over from his antique store."

Jeremy smiled. "My wife, Grace, suggested it might be something to put outside the bakery or hang on the wall. The bicycle is a JC Higgins from the 1950s. If you want, I could paint and fix it up for you."

"That would be awesome," Olivia said. "Thanks, Jeremy. Mom, what do you think?"

"I love the idea." Crystal ran her hand along the frame. "Were you thinking teal or pink or some other color?"

"Maybe a pretty teal since the crawdad in the mural is wearing a teal apron." She turned to Jeremy. "Could you do that? I mean, paint the bike for me?"

"Sure. I could have it done for you in a couple of days. By the way, the display wall box you ordered for the old kitchen items is ready. I'll bring it over when I have everything finished. I also have a lady who makes stained glass to sell in the shop. Would you want her name? It might be something you could put over the transom over your front door." At her nod, he took out his phone and texted Olivia the number.

"Thanks, Jeremy, for everything. Let me know how much the charge is, and please bring me the bill."

He nodded and rolled the bike out the door.

Olivia turned to Crystal. "And guess what else? Aunt Katherine is going to put up a stripped teal and white awning over the front door."

Crystal matched Olivia's big smile. "That sounds perfect."

As Olivia walked back to check on the movers, Eric turned to Crystal. "It looks like everything is falling into place. The town is buzzing about the bakery opening soon. Oh, and Marcus stopped by Doohickeys yesterday and seemed very interested that Olivia would be running the place. He asked me if she had a boyfriend."

"He did, did he? I'll be interested to see when he stops by to visit."

Grinning, Eric nudged her with his elbow. "Our town is a very friendly place." He leaned toward her ear. "Want to go on another late-night raid with me? One of the widows, Ms. Norma, looked slightly down when she entered my store the other day."

"I would love that." Crystal kept her voice low. "What were you thinking?"

He leaned so close she could smell his minty, fresh breath. "Maybe we could plant some mums around her mailbox. She used to have pretty flowers, but I think her arthritis is keeping her from being able to take care of her yard the way she used to. We could wait until next week since you're still getting settled."

"I'm ready whenever you want to do it."

"Great. I'll give you a few days to get settled, and then I can take you out for dinner. Then we could head back to my place for dessert, wait until the town quieted down for the night, and then sneak over to her house."

"Sounds like a plan." Crystal really wanted to do a happy dance. "You've given me a burst of energy, so I better return to unpacking."

"I'm here to help all day. Just tell me what to do, and I'll get it done."

Crystal hurried up the stairs to the apartment as Eric followed behind. In the kitchen, they unpacked and arranged the kitchen items. As they worked, they talked about their childhood memories and the fun things they used to do as kids in Crawdad Beach.

Finished with the kitchen, they moved to her bedroom and unloaded the big hanging clothes boxes. Eric stayed with her, and in no time, her clothes were in the closet or dresser, the bed made, and the boxes emptied.

With a satisfied smile, Crystal glanced around her new room. "I feel like we've been in speed mode getting everything done so quickly."

"We do make a good team."

It was a good thing the door was open, and the apartment was full of family members, or she would have been tempted to plant a big kiss on his cute grin. "We better go see what else needs to be done."

His gaze drifted to her lips. "I think that would be a very wise idea."

Even though he was sore from helping Crystal get settled, Eric whistled as he walked to his house. Nine o'clock at night, and the town was already quiet. Before he turned the corner, he turned back to look at where she and her daughter were staying. He was grateful he could spend most of the day with her, and it was nice knowing she was here to stay. It gave him renewed hope for the future.

If nothing else, he had another friend in town. He did still worry about her. She didn't say anything, but he would catch her rubbing at her hip. Hopefully, whatever pain she felt was only a pulled muscle and nothing serious.

Eric spotted and waved at Gabriel, Crawdad Beach's plainclothes policeman. Eric felt rather proud of himself that he had spotted the man. Even though Gabriel stood six feet three, for some reason, he had a talent for almost making himself invisible. Between the chief and Gabriel patrolling the streets, their little town didn't have any major problems.

Eric picked up his pace. Gadget would probably be dancing since it had been hours since he had come home to let her out. His pup made happy barking sounds as Eric unlocked his door. She ran to his arms as soon as he opened the door.

Cuddling Gadget against his chest, he pet her soft fur. Letting her outside, he checked his cell. Messages were waiting from both of his daughters. Hoping everything was okay, he read the texts and listened to their voicemails. He smiled and felt a little light-headed. His daughters were both engaged to be married. Even though the girls were two years apart, they had always been best friends. It didn't surprise him that they would get engaged on the same day.

He called each daughter and listened as they shared about how their boyfriends had asked them to marry them and all their plans for the years ahead. As happy as he was for his daughters, he was sad they wouldn't settle in Crawdad Beach. Both of the girl's fiancés had jobs in Research Triangle Park, so after graduation, they would live in Raleigh, North Carolina. At least that was still within driving distance.

After the calls ended, he received a flurry of videos and photos from when each boyfriend proposed. Eric smiled and wiped away happy tears. The young men had come to him privately the last time they visited and asked if it would be okay to marry his daughters. Eric had been surprised they had been kind enough to seek his permission since he wasn't sure if the younger generation still did things like that. Eric had tearfully and happily given them each his blessing. He couldn't have picked better young men for his daughters to marry.

At Gadget's bark, Eric remembered to let her inside. He sank onto the couch, and his pup curled in his lap. How he wished Amy was here to celebrate with all of them. He and Amy had raised their daughters to be God reliant, independent, and self-sufficient. He knew his daughters would be fine.

As happy as he was for his daughters, a deep sadness cloaked his shoulders. Soon, both his girls would be living their own lives as married women. He was happy for them and excited for their next steps, but their new beginnings meant a very lonely future for him.

Bible verses came to mind about God being with His children and never leaving or forsaking them. He knew all those verses and had memorized many of them when Amy fought to stay alive. God's promises were great, but that didn't mean life was easy. Pain, illness, and heartache were part of everyone's journey. He knew that all too well.

When his dad passed away from a heart attack, Eric had a hard enough time with his own grief, but his mom never did get over losing her husband. She had passed away within nine months of his dad's death. Seeing her grieve made Eric believe someone really could die of a broken heart.

Trying to tamp down a growing headache and the sadness surrounding him, he rubbed his forehead. As an only child, he had a good life growing up in Crawdad Beach with loving parents. But they were gone, his wife was gone, and now his daughters would only come home for brief visits. He'd be gaining sons-in-law, but his daughters would no longer be his little girls.

Gadget whimpered and stared up at him with her big brown eyes. Did she sense his sadness? Eric rubbed the little dog. "Thanks, I'm okay. My girls are getting married." The words choked on his tightening throat.

He should be thrilled. Instead, he was sitting here thinking about himself. He should be thinking of his girls. So, what was he supposed to do as a bride's dad? Especially two brides? Was he supposed to pay for something besides maybe a wedding dress for the girls? Did he have to pay for dinner, reception, cake, and stuff like that?

His headache surged to full force. Why did Amy have to die? He couldn't even call his mom. He was an orphan, widower, of two girls who would need weddings. What was he supposed to do?

Eric rubbed the back of his neck. He needed to get a grip. Be a man. He took a deep breath and blew it out. Maybe he could ask the Crawdad Beach Prayer Team for help. There were enough praying women in town, and surely someone would take pity on him and tell him what he needed to do. He took a calming breath.

Before he continued panicking, he probably should check with his girls. No telling what they wanted for their weddings. Would they come back here or get married there? Would it be an inside or outside wedding? Thank goodness, he and Amy had put money aside in a mutual fund to save for his daughter's big days. Last he checked, there should be plenty to help make the day memorable for them both.

Tomorrow, he would start asking around what he needed to do. Gloria would be a big help since her three daughters were married. Maybe Crystal would even have some ideas. Okay. He could do this: be the dad of the brides.

Eric tried not to worry about whatever was coming. He needed to put together a plan for a late-night raid with Crystal. He'd buy some of the mums he had at his store and put together a small bag of dirt and tools in a bag to carry. He'd take her to dinner, and then he needed to make something for dessert. Since Crystal's daughter was a pastry chef, it would be hard to impress her. Maybe he wouldn't even try and just buy something fancy from the grocery store.

Either way, it would be nice to see Crystal again. Other than his time with Amy, many of his best memories had been with Crystal. If his prayers were answered, they might make new and even better memories.

# *Chapter 10*

Heart thumping in her chest and face hurting from smiling so much, Crystal clutched the tray of flowers as she and Eric hurried down the quiet street. With a big canvas bag slung over his shoulders, he carried the tools and supplies needed for their late-night raid. It seemed most people had gone to bed even though it was only ten o'clock at night. Because of the full moon, porch lights, and streetlights, they had no trouble seeing the mailbox.

She'd already had a great evening with Eric. They'd eaten dinner at Tiddlywinks, had dessert at his house, and then talked until time for their late-night raid.

Stopping at the lady's mailbox, Crystal placed the flowers on the grass as Eric set the canvas bag beside them. He took out his garden tools and a bag of potting soil and handed her a small trowel.

His knees creaked and popped as he stooped to dig around the mailbox. Crystal leaned down to help, but her hip caught. Gasping, she stifled a giggle. "Oh my goodness, we sound like two old people between your creaky knees and my hip."

Eric gave a quiet laugh as he worked to prepare the area. "Are you okay?".

Still giggling, she rubbed the sore spot. "Yes, I'll be fine."

They removed the old, dead flowers, and new ones were placed in the fresh garden soil. As Eric stood, his knees creaked again and kept creaking as he moved around to put the tools and dead debris in his sack. Crystal giggled and couldn't stop giggling. Even Eric got tickled.

They cleaned up the area, and when finished, they kept trying not to laugh too loud as they ran back to his house. By the time they arrived, she could barely breathe.

Eric put his key in his front door and stopped. "Want to come in to wash up and have a nightcap?" At her surprised expression, he clarified. "I mean a cup of decaf coffee."

"That would be great." She followed him inside and they both stopped to pet his little fluff ball of a puppy with a crooked tail.

He picked up his little dog. "I'll take Gadget outside for a few minutes if you want to wash up."

After cleaning off the dirt from their hands, they took their coffee mugs, moved to his back deck, and sat in chairs facing the yard. String lights over their head shimmied in the gentle breeze. Crickets chirped and then quieted as Gadget sniffed and explored the grass.

Crystal and Eric talked in soft tones about the people they knew and the things that had changed over the years.

Crystal swatted a mosquito buzzing close to her ear, then checked the time. "Yikes, it's midnight. I need to get home."

Eric grinned at her. "Going to turn into a pumpkin?"

"No, but I don't want Olivia worried or think we've been doing something we shouldn't be doing."

He chuckled. "It sounds like when we were in high school. You never wanted to disappoint your parents."

"No, I didn't." She gave a contented sigh. "Thank you for always being a gentleman and making sure I was home at least a few minutes before curfew."

"I might have behaved appropriately," One of Eric's eyebrows raised. "but that didn't mean I didn't think about being less than gentlemanly at times."

Heat enveloped Crystal's body. She didn't want him to know she had several thoughts of her own. Sitting with Eric and having such a fun evening with him made her thoughts go in all sorts of directions that could lead in a way she shouldn't let them lead.

Eric stood and pulled her to her feet, and his gaze rested on her lips. She was close enough to smell a hint of his cologne. Oh, she knew what he wanted, and she wanted to kiss him too. Memories of the many nights long ago when they had kissed until their lips were sore. They had never taken things too far, and for that, she would forever be grateful. Now, they were both adults. His chest strong and firm, and his lips looked so sweet, she could get in trouble way too fast.

He gently pulled away. "I hate to say it, but I better get you home."

She took a deep breath and tried to steady herself. "Yes, you have. I'm thinking some very unladylike thoughts."

Eric cleared his throat and nodded. "If we start dating again, being good might be a little more difficult. If you know what I mean."

"Oh, I know what you mean. And yes, it's going to be very difficult."

"I may hire a chaperone." He pointed to his little dog.

Crystal laughed. "I don't know that Gadget would be very helpful. And hiring a personal chaperone would be difficult. The whole town would be talking, wouldn't they?"

"They probably already are since we ate together at Tiddlywinks." He took her hand in his and moved closer. "So, would you consider dating a guy like me?"

She gulped. Could she risk her heart again? Was it too soon? Then again, she was with her handsome friend Eric. He had always been a good guy, always a gentleman, and now she had a chance to dive into a relationship. But what if it didn't work out? What would happen since they lived in a small town? The what-ifs ran rampant, ramming, pushing, and shoving through her mind.

He gave her forehead a gentle kiss. "Your brain is on overdrive. I didn't mean for it to be a difficult question.

Crystal, I've always cared for you. If things don't look like they are working out between us, we can still be friends."

She wrinkled her nose. "Don't you think that's easier said than done in real life?"

"With some people, yes. But I don't see that happening with us. To be honest, I'm a little scared, too, but I don't want to miss the opportunity to see if we have a shot at a long-term relationship."

"It sounds scary, frightening, and wonderful." She looked in his beautiful blue eyes. "So, you're thinking long-term?"

"I'm not looking for anything other than the possibility of marriage."

Crystal couldn't help but think of a scene from a funny movie. "Mawige is a sewious thing."

Eric busted out a laugh. "I love that line. That was a great movie! Yes, mawige is sewious. So, you up for moving forward?"

"Yes, but do you think other people will think we're moving too fast by saying we're dating? I haven't been in town that long."

"We're both in our forties, and it's not like anyone can lecture us that we're too young or have no idea what might happen. I hate that we've both lost our spouses. I'm not trying to rush, but I don't want to miss a day with you. We had a blast together in high school, and I know it won't be the same, but I've missed having fun with my very good friend."

"I've missed you too. Tonight was hilarious. Made me feel like a kid again."

"Yeah, me too." Eric took her hand and kissed it. "So, Crystal Doss Baker, will you be my steady date?"

"I would be honowed. Sewiously honowed."

Crystal felt seventeen again as Eric held her hand while they walked to her apartment.

Outside the building door, he stopped and hugged her. "Thanks for a great evening."

"Thank you." Feeling his heart's steady beat, she rested her head on his shoulders. "It was so much fun. We'll have to do another late-night raid."

"I'll keep my ears open for other opportunities. How about you let me take you to one of the seafood places over by the ocean next time? Say, next Friday evening?"

"I'd like that."

"It's a date." With a sigh, he stepped back. "I better go."

"Yes, you better go." With a smile, she unlocked the door and said goodnight.

Trying to be as quiet as possible, she crossed the creaky floor, went up the creaky stairs, and opened the apartment door.

A flash of light momentarily blinded her.

"Where have you been?" Glaring, Olivia stood next to the light switch. "It's after midnight."

Crystal laughed. "You're kidding, right?"

"No, I was worried."

"I'm sorry." Crystal tried to keep a straight face as she walked to her bedroom. "You knew I was going out with Eric."

Olivia followed. "I didn't think you'd be gone this long."

"We were having fun."

A disgusted look crossed her daughter's face as she held up her hand. "I do not want to hear about that."

"Oh, my goodness. We didn't do anything. It was strictly a G-rated date." Crystal smiled as she removed her shoes and put them in her closet. "I can't believe we're having this discussion."

"The building creaks and moans and groans." Olivia's eyes got watery. "It's kind of creepy at night when you aren't here."

"Oh, honey. I'm sorry. Crawdad Beach is a safe little town. If it would make you feel better, Katherine said she had prewired the building for a security system and cameras. So, it wouldn't take her long to set us up with everything."

"Good. I'd like that. And you need to let me know when you'll be late."

"Yes, ma'am. I promise to do better next time." She studied her daughter's face. "Are you okay? Is something else going on?" Crystal sat on her bed and patted the bedspread.

Olivia plopped on the bed and crossed her arms. "It's nothing. I just, it's all new. It's good, but it's weird starting over, and no offense, strange living again with my mom. Things are so different, and tonight, while you were gone, I was thinking about stuff. And it made me sad in some ways and really excited in other ways."

"This is a big move. You're starting over, and it's okay to grieve a little for the life you thought you would have. But I just know you're going to do great running this bakery. The family is here to help, and you'll make new friends. And Marcus sure is cute."

"Oh, Mom. I don't need another boyfriend. I'm through with men."

"Well, we'll not worry about that right now. Grieve what is gone, but be open to what is next. God is always good, and His plans are the best."

Olivia frowned as she stood. "Good night, Mom. Sleep tight." She shut the door behind her.

Crystal sighed. She wished and prayed she could talk to Olivia about God without her getting angry. So many positive things were happening that proved and showed God's love toward them both. How many young women would have the opportunity to open a bakery without worrying about big bills to pay? And as much as Olivia was angry about Geoff, Crystal believed God's grace rescued her from that bad relationship.

Well, whatever happened next, she needed to be patient and continue loving and praying for Olivia.

# *Chapter 11*

Eric hummed as he swept Doohickeys old wood floor. Being with Crystal and dating Crystal made him feel like a teenager again. This morning, as he got ready for work, he played some of the music they used to listen to when they were in high school. He was surprised at how much he did not like anymore.

He'd been thinking back and realized he and Crystal had spent most of their time with the church youth group, school groups, family get-togethers, or hanging out at the beach. His long hours working at Doohickeys helping his dad had limited his free time.

The store's front door banged open. Chester yelled an apology as he wrestled it closed in the stiff wind. "It's trampoline flying weather out there."

Eric chuckled at the comment. "It is crazy windy this morning. How can I help you today?"

"Well, we're almost done with our table projects, but we need more varnish. Just got a few more to finish." Chester glanced at a written note in his hands and read for a few moments. "And Jeremy asked if you could order some pre-woven cane. He said you should be able to find it in sheets by the inch, and he also needs some cane spline."

"So, you guys are fixing up chairs with cane seats?"

"Yep, we think they'll look pretty spiffy over at Rolling in the Dough." Chester smiled. "I just love that name. You'll have to stop by this evening after you close. It's coming together. Tess painted a big mural with a bakery crawdad that's cute as a button." Chester paused and scratched his chin. "That saying is kind of strange, isn't it? I don't know that I would ever say a button is cute. You know, there are sure a lot of sayings we say that don't make much sense. Like when someone says they will keep an eye out for you. Do you realize how wrong that sounds? I'm not taking out my eye for anyone."

Eric chuckled as he typed on his computer. "While you ponder those facts, I'll place your order. I assume you guys want it rushed, right?"

"That'd be great. We've got to get everything finished real soon. Olivia's already started baking mouth-watering desserts and sharing samples with friends and family."

"I definitely need to get over there."

Chester's grin turned mischievous. "Crystal sure was starry-eyed and in a happy mood this morning. Wonder what the cause of that might be?" He cast a knowing look at Eric.

Eric shrugged one shoulder. "Maybe she's just happy to be back in Crawdad Beach."

"I'm sure she is. Probably because of a certain widower who looks pretty starry-eyed himself." Chester gave a deep chuckle, then turned serious. "On a more semi-serious note, bring your lawnmower to the Main Street sidewalk today at six o'clock this evening. Lucy's son is bringing her home this evening. As a salute to her return, all the Crawdadians will line up and start their lawnmowers as she passes by."

"What a great idea. I'll make sure to bring mine for the celebration. I'll rush your order to get here sometime tomorrow."

"Sammie!" Chester called. "Make sure you come with your lawnmower for Lucy's homecoming."

"Yes, sir." Sammie, who had been in the stockroom, walked toward them. "I'll be there."

"Thanks, son." Chester patted the young man on the shoulder. "Tell your folks hello for me. Are they feeling better?"

"Yes, sir. They're both doing much better. That flu bug hit them hard."

"Maybelline will be bringing a casserole by this evening."

"Thank you," Sammie said. "Much appreciated. We all love your wife's cooking."

"Me too." Chester smiled. "You take good care of yourself, okay?"

"I'll do that. Thanks."

After Chester paid for his purchase and left, Eric turned to Sammie. "I didn't know your parents were sick."

Sammie's gaze dropped to the floor, and he shuffled his feet. "I don't want to bother you with stuff like that. You're the boss."

"And you're my employee and friend. Please never feel like you can't come to me, okay?"

"Thanks. I'll remember that." Sammie gave him a grin and went back to work.

Eric stood at the counter. Obviously, he needed to pay more attention to what was happening with his employees. He should have known about Sammie's parents being sick.

Gloria peeked out of the back office. "What's this I hear about Lucy?"

"She's coming home this evening," Eric said as he walked to where she stood. "We're lining up along Main Street and starting our lawnmowers as her son drives her by."

"Oh, that's a perfect way to welcome her home. I'll call my husband and let him know."

Eric stopped her before she returned to her desk. "Are you doing okay? Family okay?"

"Yes, everything's fine." Gloria gave him an inquisitive look. "Why?"

"I just found out Sammie's parents had been sick, and I feel bad I didn't even know."

Gloria patted his arm. "You have been a little distracted by sweet Crystal's move to town."

The back of his neck heated. "That obvious?"

"Oh, yes, it is." She grinned and nodded. "You two do make a good pair. I thought so even when you were dating her in high school."

"She is pretty special." Eric gave Gloria an apologetic look. "But Amy was, too."

"Yes, Amy was. And you don't need to worry that I, or anyone else, might think you'll forget her. We all loved Amy, but sometimes God blesses us with new beginnings."

Eric cleared his tightened throat. "Thanks. Please pray I don't run ahead of what God has planned."

Gloria smiled. "Eric, so many people in this town are praying for you and Crystal. You'll be fine."

Eric grinned as he walked away. He knew he was in good hands; he just hoped he didn't do anything to mess things up.

Excitement building, Crystal stood by her family and waved at Eric across the street in front of Doohickeys. It looked like almost all of the town had lined up with their lawnmowers on the sidewalk beside Main Street. Even little children had their toy lawnmowers ready.

"I can't believe this place." Olivia's smile beamed as she glanced back and forth. "This is amazing."

"I know, what a sweet group of people to be ready to welcome home Lawnmower Lucy."

Chester swiped at his eyes. "Reminds me of when Maybelline came home from her hip surgery. Since she was the librarian, the townspeople lined the streets with books open in a salute."

Maybelline's bouffant hairdo trembled along with her lip. "It was the sweetest thing. So thoughtful."

Chester gave Crystal a mischievous grin. "It's a good thing we haven't had anyone bitten by a snake. No telling what the welcome home committee would do."

"They're coming!" The shout came from a little boy further down the street.

People rushed to start up their lawnmowers and stood to salute. Their windows open, Lucy's son slowly drove the car as she waved and clapped in glee.

When the car turned off Main Street, people shut off their lawnmower engines and stood around talking and visiting.

Olivia ran off to visit with her cousins.

Crystal's eyes got all misty, and she retreated to their building. Why had she waited so long to come back to Crawdad Beach?

Her dad followed. "Why the sad face?"

"I just wish we had come here sooner."

His tender blue-eyes gazed at her. "I wish you had, too, but we must trust that God's timing is perfect."

Crystal stood by the front window and watched the townspeople continue to visit. Eric held up his hand in another wave, then turned to go. She should have stayed out there celebrating and enjoying being with family and friends.

She sighed. "Is God's timing perfect, even when people get stubborn?"

"No matter what happens or happened, God knows."

"I read a meme on social media that God has already factored in our stupidity."

"I am very grateful God is gracious."

Crystal watched as Olivia laughed with other family members. It was so long since she'd seen Olivia happy like that. "Maybe I should have moved here right after Sean died. Maybe things would be different with Olivia, and she wouldn't be so mad at God."

"Perhaps. But we don't know what is happening behind the scenes. I know you've prayed many times about whether or not you should move here and never felt God had opened that door."

"That's true, but still I wonder." She missed years of being with her family. Even though her other siblings were spread across the country, Crystal would have had more time with her mom and Uncle Kenneth before they passed. But what worried her the most was whether Olivia would have been better off if they had moved here sooner.

"Someday, we will see the big picture." Her dad's gentle voice interrupted her thoughts. "I take great comfort in the verses that say that a man plans his way, but the Lord directs his steps, and God's ways are not our ways."

Crystal blew out a breath. "I want to do things God's way, but it's so hard to know the way, you know?"

He nodded. "God is patient, kind, and loving, and promises to guide and lead His children."

"I just wish God would give me a plan, a day-by-day agenda, what to do, where to go, and how to do everything I need to do."

"We have the Bible for instruction, comfort, and guidance, and we have prayer to talk and listen to God, and we have to walk by faith and not by sight."

"I read my Bible, and I pray, and still feel like I stumble in the dark most of the time."

"We all feel that sometimes."

"Even you?"

"Yes, even me. I'm not perfect, and I need God's help at every moment of my day."

"But you always seem to have it together and have a hotline to God."

"Oh, Crystal. I don't have it all together, but I do know that God's love is unfailing, and we can come to Him day or night with every question, doubt, and fear. God promises to lead and guide us. He is a forgiving God when we come to Him for forgiveness. And God can not lie, so

His promises are true. And another verse is that He beckons us to come to Him, and He will give us rest. Whatever is making you out of rest, read your Bible, go to God, talk to Him, and listen and let His loving truth wrap you in His rest."

# *Chapter 12*

Crystal sat in the doctor's examination room. They had already taken an X-ray of her hip, and now she waited to hear the results.

She was surprisingly calm. Last night, she had stayed up reading her chronological Bible. So many questions about why things happened in the Bible made more sense when she could read the historical order. The true-life accounts of Biblical people showed over and over God's love and desire to guide and direct them. Even when people failed and messed up, God's mercy and grace lifted them back on their feet and on the right path. That comforted her because she was not perfect and needed forgiveness and all the help God could give her. She had spent time in prayer about the past, prayed about the future, and prayed about this appointment. And peace had come. She still had no idea what was next, but she could trust God, and He would help her through whatever she went through. And best of all, Crystal knew that God loved Olivia with an unfailing love, and He would continue to draw her back to Him.

The doctor entered the room, sat at his computer, and opened where the X-ray showed on the screen. "You have a dark shadow right here," he pointed at the area and turned his attention toward her. "Has your hip ever been injured?"

Crystal stared at the X-ray as she tried to think. "About twenty years ago, I had a bone spur on the side of my hip that had shredded my tendons and ligaments to the point the surgeon said they looked like spaghetti. He cut out the mangled area, ground down the hip bone, and then pulled the remaining tendons and ligaments to attach to my hip bone. It's been years, and it still hurts and gives me trouble if I sleep on that side."

The doctor surveyed the X-ray again. "It's possible your blood flow was compromised. You may have avascular necrosis, which means your hip bone may not be getting the blood supply it needs, which could cause the bone to die."

Light-headed, Crystal blinked to steady herself. "That doesn't sound good."

"Don't worry. I'll order an MRI to get a better look. Whatever it is, we'll get you fixed up. I'll have my nurse call and get you in for that test. Once it's finished, we can sit down again to discuss the options."

On autopilot, Crystal thanked the doctor, checked out, and sat in her car. If his diagnosis were correct, she'd have to have a hip replacement. Seriously? At her age? Ugh. Growl. Argh. She was too young for that, and she didn't have time for surgery. She needed to be healthy and strong for Olivia. Good grief, they were just getting settled in Crawdad Beach.

Crystal took a calming breath. Maybe the MRI would show it was just a salsa stain and nothing serious. Her hip throbbed as though reminding her she could not continue to ignore the problem.

Should she tell her family anything? No. They didn't need to know, not yet. Tonight, she had a date with Eric. She needed to leave her worries behind and enjoy their time together.

Barely paying attention to her surroundings, Crystal drove home. She arrived at their building an hour later and walked to the downstairs kitchen.

"Hey, Mom. Look what I got today?" Olivia held up an official-looking document. "So far, I've registered for taxes, have the EIN and the LLC for the bakery, and have a business license. I've also started the applications for a food service permit, a Health Department Permit, a sales tax permit, a signage permit, and a Certificate of Occupancy. Hopefully, I'll have everything we need to open soon."

"Goodness, that's a lot. I'm proud of you for getting all that done."

"Thanks. It's been a hassle, and I couldn't have figured all this out without the Hollis's help. Since they run Tiddlywinks, they knew everything we would need here in South Carolina. Plus, even the Mayor has helped.

Living in a small town sure does have its perks. Everybody has bent over backward to get things underway."

"Crawdad Beach is a great town. Do you need money to get all these things done?"

"Nope. I've got it covered. I've been saving for years."

"You have?"

"Yes, I have." Olivia gave her a cute, smug grin. "And don't look so shocked. I have savings and a 401K with a nice amount. I started saving a portion of my income back from my very first job. As soon as the bakery starts making money, I will start paying back Grandad. "

"Look at you, all grown up."

"Seriously? I'm twenty-three. I've been adulting for years."

Crystal chuckled. "Yes, you have. I'm proud of you. Oh, and I have a date with Eric tonight, but don't worry, I plan on getting home at a decent time."

"Good. But don't worry about getting home too early. I'm going to work on a few recipes for the bakery."

Crystal went upstairs, entered her bedroom, and placed her purse on her dresser. She rubbed her throbbing hip. The timing of all of this was not good.

Why did the X-ray show something negative? If she did have a problem, could she keep everything secret? The last thing she wanted to do was worry Olivia. Crystal took a deep breath. She could do this, move forward, enjoy her time with Eric tonight, and pretend there was nothing to worry about.

Walking to her closet to pick an outfit, pain stabbed Crystal's hip. She sucked in a breath. No. Nothing to worry about at all.

# *Chapter 13*

Two hundred ten calories in one cup? Crystal sighed as she surveyed her over-filled bowl of her favorite breakfast cereal. The brand might be healthy, but why couldn't good-tasting things be low-calorie?

Last night's dinner with Eric would have gone well if not for her distracted thoughts. The restaurant he had taken her to had great seafood, and the seat next to the windows overlooking the ocean was perfect. She'd been so focused and worried about her hip problems that he had picked up on her mood.

Her stupid leg had been twitching the whole time she had thought about what might happen, and Eric had quickly guessed what was bothering her. She had told him about the doctor's visit, and he had just about jumped out of his seat. The conversation replayed in her mind.

*"You mean your hip bone is dying? Like Bo Jackson, the football player after he got hit during a football game? Wait a minute, when you were younger, you used to play pretty rough football with your older brothers."*

*"You bet I did. I'm sure I don't have anything like Bo. It's probably just a big stain from overeating salsa."*

*"Well, whatever it is, will you keep me informed? Please?"*

*"Eric, I haven't even told my family yet. I don't want anyone to worry until I really know what's going on."*

*"Alright, your secret is safe with me. But you probably should at least tell your dad. He's great at praying."*

*"I'll think about it."* Crystal reached toward him, offering her hand. *"Right now, let's enjoy our evening."*

*Eric took her hand in his and gave her a gentle squeeze.*

Crystal groaned at the memory of the hurt and concern in his expression. Even though the rest of the evening was pleasant, it seemed like a dark cloud hung over their heads. He'd brought her home right after dinner and given her a quick kiss. Was he pulling away from her? She wouldn't blame him. He'd lost his wife, and he probably didn't want to take a chance on what might happen.

"So, how was your date with Eric?"

Crystal swallowed the bite she'd been chewing and looked over her shoulder as Olivia walked toward her. "Fine. How was your evening?"

"Good. I tweaked a cookie recipe that turned out awesome." Olivia took a bowl out of the cabinet and sat across from her. "I have a few left downstairs."

"A few?"

"Yes. I had to try the cookies to make sure they were good." Olivia grinned as she poured cereal and milk into her bowl. "But, don't switch the attention to me. You need to give me details about what's happening with Eric."

"Details?"

A disgusted look crossed Olivia's face. "No, not details. I mean, is your relationship with Eric moving along?"

Crystal shrugged. "Maybe." If she could get through this hip thing.

"Well, that was a non-answer answer. So, did Grandad and Chester look into the guys you dated when you were growing up?"

"I'm not sure. I didn't date too much. Eric and I were friends more than anything."

"It must have been interesting growing up in a small town."

"There were good things and not-so-good things."

"Like what?"

Crystal wouldn't ever admit to her daughter the time she'd been caught trying to steal a puppy from their next-door neighbors. Even though she was only four at the time, she knew better. "You couldn't get away with much since everybody seemed to know everybody."

"That would be a bummer in some ways, and I guess kinda good. That time I had a flat tire at night while driving on the freeway was not fun. I wasn't sure who might stop to help and how I would get home. I'm grateful we had that auto service card I could call."

"Me too. I'm very grateful you were okay. When I was a teenager, I had a flat tire on a country road. Three men stopped to help, and I knew and trusted every one of them."

"That would be nice," Olivia said.

"It would have been, but I was on a road I shouldn't have been on." Crystal cringed at the memory.

Olivia leaned forward. "Why? Was it dangerous?"

"No, I had been driving by a person's house to see what they were doing."

"A person?"

"Okay, a friend of mine had a crush on this football player who was a senior in high school. We were sixteen, and I was driving by the guy's house."

"Checking out the guy, huh?"

"Kind of. He was having a wild party, and we had been told not to go near that place."

"Caught red-handed with a flat tire. Olivia looked far too delighted at Crystal's discomfort. "How embarrassing."

"Yes, it was. Obviously, Dad found out about it and wasn't too happy. I was grounded for quite some time."

Olivia tsked. "My mother, the wild woman. I'm so ashamed."

"I'll try and behave. So, what's on the agenda today?"

"I'm going to work on a recipe to share for taste-testing."

"You are an amazing pastry chef, and I can't wait until the bakery opens and you can share your talent."

"Thanks, mom. Tess is coming over to help after she drops the twins off at school."

Crystal's phone signaled an incoming call. She glanced at the local area code. Rising to her feet, she tried to act nonchalant as she answered and walked to her bedroom.

The nurse from the doctor's office told her the MRI was scheduled for the following day and told her where she needed to go for the procedure. Crystal took notes, thanked the woman, and pulled up her phone's map program to chart her course. At least she wouldn't have to wait long for the MRI, but what would she tell Olivia?

Trying to act upbeat, she walked back to the kitchen.

Grateful Olivia was talking on her phone, Crystal finished her cereal and loaded her bowl in the dishwasher.

Olivia sat her phone down and looked up. "That was Tess. She'll be over soon."

She gave her daughter a tight hug. "I love you. You know that?"

"Yeah, I love you too." Olivia squirmed out of the embrace. "I better get downstairs and get things ready."

"Don't forget, Katherine and her electrician are coming this morning to install the security system. Eric is also bringing the shelving to install in the storage room, and the office equipment should be here this afternoon."

"Great, that's right. Everything is coming together." Olivia thanked her and ran down the stairs.

Crystal sent up a prayer of thanks that she didn't have to say anything about her doctor's appointment. With everything falling into place for the bakery, surely whatever was going on with her hip wouldn't be a problem.

From his work van, Eric grabbed a box of unassembled six-tier heavy-duty metal shelving for Crystal's building. They had ordered five gleaming seventy-eight-inch high and forty-eight-inch wide adjustable shelves for their storage area.

Crystal looked super cute wearing a much-used old t-shirt and shorts as she stood beside him, "Are you sure you don't need my help?"

"No, I've got it." He tried to ignore her shapely tan legs as he hiked the heavy box on his shoulder and adjusted to distribute the weight. "But do you mind grabbing my tool belt?"

She picked it up and wrapped it around her tiny hips. "I could use one like this."

"You used to have a pretty nice one when you were a kid. Of course, you did draw flowers and hearts on yours."

"Unfortunately, that one is no longer with me, but I still have a good collection of tools." She nodded toward a stack of boxes on the back wall. "I haven't unpacked any of them yet." She smiled and shimmied her eyebrows. "Not when I have a handyman on call."

"Eric Reed is here for your every need."

A blush colored Crystal's pretty face. "I'll remember that fact."

At her saucy grin, he cleared his throat. "Just show me where you want everything installed."

Crystal opened the storage area and led him inside. "Katherine and her electrician are working on installing the security system, and Tess and Olivia are working in the kitchen. Everything is coming together."

He set the box on the back wall. "I'm impressed how fast the renovation has gone."

"I know. Me too. I'll open the boxes," Crystal said as she handed him his tool belt, then held up a box cutter. "and if you have time, we can put the shelving together."

"Of course, I have time. That's why I'm here with my tool belt." Eric leaned toward her and kept his voice quiet. "Any updates on your hip?"

"I have an MRI scheduled for tomorrow morning."

"I'll be praying for you."

Her big brown eyes gazed up at him. She whispered her thanks, then knelt and opened the boxes.

"Is someone going with you for the appointment?"

Crystal shook her head and avoided his concerned look.

"Why not? I can go with you if everyone is busy."

"It's not that. I'd just rather do this on my own."

Eric got down beside her and helped her take out the parts. "Why would you do that? We all need help at times."

"I know. I just... it's silly for anyone to go with me. They'd have to sit in an uncomfortable waiting room."

He let out an exasperated sigh. "You always wanted to be the tough one."

She straightened her back. "Excuse me?"

"Crystal, even when we were kids, you played football with the guys. Using every tool known to man, you built projects with your sister. And remember the time you fell off your bicycle and split your chin wide open? You still have a scar because you wouldn't go to the doctor."

"I don't have scars; they are my courage badges."

Eric pulled her to her feet and wrapped her in a tight hug. "You don't have to be so tough all the time. Please let your family, let me, let us help you."

"I'll think about it." Her voice was muffled against his chest.

He loosened his grip. "Do more than think about it. Please have someone with you."

She pulled away from his embrace and went back to opening boxes.

Eric inwardly groaned. He had upset her. Why was she being stubborn about this? Having someone to drive her, or at least keep her company on the drive, made sense to him. Then again, maybe she needed the time alone. Eric walked back to his work van and pulled out another box. Maybe he shouldn't push her so hard. But blast it, he cared about her and knew her family loved her. Why was she making it so difficult to take care of her?

Eric stepped aside as Jeremy's work truck backed in next to him.

Knick Knacks antique store's tall, brown-haired owner hopped out of the truck. "Hey, you need help?"

"Nah, I got it. You delivering something?"

"Yep, Olivia picked out a desk, shelves, and a file cabinet for her office."

"Let me put these away, and I'll give you a hand."

"Thanks. I appreciate it." Jeremy grabbed one of the shelving boxes and put it on his shoulder. "Show me where this goes."

Eric nodded his thanks and walked back to the storage area. "Look who I found."

Crystal grinned at the young man. "Hi, Jeremy. Olivia said you were bringing the office furniture today."

"Yes, ma'am." He glanced at Eric. "We'll get it in for you in a few minutes."

"Great," Crystal said. "I'll go get Olivia for you." Without acknowledging Eric's presence, she hurried out of the room.

Jeremy ignored the apparent slight by Crystal. "I'll help you bring in the other boxes you brought."

In no time, he and Jeremy had the boxes in the storage room, then moved on to bring in the office furniture.

Olivia, Tess, and Crystal waited in the office, and Olivia directed them to where everything was to be placed.

Once they finished, Eric returned to the storage room to finish putting together the shelving. Crystal wouldn't even look at him. Eric rubbed the back of his neck. He knew he was in trouble, but he wouldn't apologize. She needed to realize that having other people help her was good for her and them. Crystal could continue to ignore him, but he wouldn't back down. Being the only male in the house as his daughters grew up, he understood the silent treatment, and he knew how to silently fight back.

With the sound of women visiting, talking, and laughing, Eric continued getting the shelving assembled and placed against the room's walls. He stepped back and admired the gleaming shelves ready for whatever they needed for the bakery.

Olivia peeked in the door. "Those are great. Thanks, Mr. Eric. I appreciate your help."

"My pleasure." He gathered his tool belt. "I need to get back to the store. Feel free to call if you need anything."

She gave him a sweet smile. "Will do. Thanks again."

Eric didn't bother looking for Crystal. Maybe he would check in on her in a few days. Or better yet, he would wait to see if she would contact him.

# *Chapter 14*

The doctor greeted Crystal as he walked into the room. "The good news is, your MRI shows that your hip bones look okay. However, the radiologist believes the dark shadow is a lipoma, a benign, fatty tissue tumor." He opened a page on his computer that showed a diagram of the bones and nerves in the hip area. "From what we can see on the MRI, the tumor is large and sitting next to two nerves and putting pressure on other areas. I'll recommend a surgeon to get things rolling."

"Okay. Thanks, I guess. I'm relieved I won't need a hip replacement or anything like that. It would be good to get out whatever that thing is because it's getting more painful during the day and harder and harder to sleep at night."

He took off his glasses and nodded. "That makes sense since sleeping positions cause more compression and would intensify your pain. I'll make sure you have pain medication and muscle relaxers until this problem is resolved. I'll have my nurse call to get you in to see the surgeon."

Crystal thanked the doctor, went through the motions again of checking out, and then started her journey back to Crawdad Beach. Hopefully, they were correct, and the tumor was benign. But what if it was the big C?

No, she couldn't think like that. There was no way she had cancer. She refused that thought. She had to think of the best scenario, not the worst. The surgeon would remove the tumor, and the pain would be gone, and she'd be able to dance to her heart's content.

But, now that she knew she needed surgery, she probably should tell her family. The first place she needed to stop was at her dad's place. He would know how to advise her. Whatever happened next, she needed his prayers.

An hour later, Crystal stood in her dad's den. She'd told him about her pain and the diagnosis. "Dad, what am I going to tell Olivia? She's already mad at God for taking Sean; what if something happens to me? Even if the tumor is benign and quickly removed, is she going to freak out that I have to have surgery?"

He gently hugged her against his chest, his heartbeat slow and steady. "It's going to be okay." He gently nudged her face up to look at him. "Whatever God has in store, it will be okay."

"But what if it's not okay?"

Her dad tilted Crystal's face up to look at him. "Thinking the worst-case scenario isn't going to help anyone."

"I know. But we prayed for healing, and Sean still died. We prayed that Mom would be healed, and she still died. What if something happens to me? I'm not afraid of dying; I just don't want it to be a painful process. And I don't want Olivia to have to go through losing another parent." She shifted out of his embrace and sat on the couch. Her leg twitched, itching for dance relief. "I just want to be prepared for whatever happens."

Her dad sat next to her. "None of us can ever be fully prepared. Life is painful at times, but God will help you through. He's already factored in whatever is coming next in your life. There's a bigger plan and purpose in everything."

"I know. Romans eight twenty-eight, God works all things out for the good." She didn't mean to raise her voice. Crystal gave him an apologetic look.

"It's okay to be upset and even afraid." He patted her hand. "But, there's more than just that verse; the next one reminds us that through our difficulties, God's good is conforming us to the image of His Son."

"Oh, wait. So it's not just the good we want, like me wanting to be healed, and the good things we want to happen?"

Her dad nodded. "Right. God's good is bigger than our earthly comfort. His good is for eternal purposes to help us become more like His beloved Son, Jesus Christ."

Crystal blew out a breath. "How did you do it, Dad? How did you stay positive even after all you went through as a kid and then losing Mom? I know it hasn't been easy."

"No, it wasn't. Crystal, there were times I was angry with God. I never knew my father, and I was only four when my mother told me she was going to the store but never returned. Yet God took care of me by providing a loving home with my adoptive parents. God was, and is, my heavenly Father, and He is always good, even when bad things happen. When your mom died, God's comfort held me close when I wept. When you lost Sean, God was there for all of us."

Warmth lined her eyelids as tears threatened to escape. "I'm sorry. I didn't mean to bring up painful memories. I am a little scared. The tumor is pretty big and sitting in an area with major veins and arteries pressing against everything."

"We will pray the surgeon can remove it without any problems."

"I hope so. It's getting more painful every day. What are we going to do about the bakery? It will be finished soon, and Olivia is itching to get started."

"There's no rush on when the bakery opens. Once you talk to Olivia, the timing will become clear. I will be praying for you. And one other thing: How best can I help encourage you?"

Surprised by his question, Crystal ran her hand through her hair. "I guess. Prayer is appreciated. As for encouragement? I'm not sure."

Her dad's gentle gaze rested on her. "I read a quote once from J. R. Miller that said, we must try to make our sick friend braver to endure his sufferings."

"That's an interesting perspective. Most of us pray to escape suffering, not be brave enough to endure it."

"I agree." He nodded. "Let me put it this way. If you were running a marathon, would you want your friends and family to stay at the starting gate, praying that you would get out of the race as quickly as possible? Or would you prefer having them come alongside you as you ran, praying for you and with you, encouraging and cheering you on to finish strong?"

Crystal could picture herself hobbling along, trying to run a race. "I need all the help I can get. Prayers and encouragement would be the best so that I can keep going whatever happens."

Her dad gave her arm a gentle squeeze. "Praying for others helps in wonderful spiritual ways we can't even fathom. Reading the Bible is another great way to receive encouragement. Some definitions of encouragement are to inspire with hope, courage, or confidence. Therefore, we will come alongside you to provide prayer, encouragement, and help where needed. We will be with you through whatever comes next."

"Thank you, Dad. I love you."

"I love you, too. Remember, in everything we go through, there is a lesson to be learned. God said He gives treasures in the darkness. Sometimes, what we go through helps us grow closer to God, and sometimes it's also for others. Think about the Bible's true-life stories, Job's suffering, or all that Paul went through. I read their stories, which helps me be braver because I can read the big picture. Now, we only see a small part of what is happening and don't know the future."

"That's true. Like David conquering Goliath, Daniel in the lion's den, and so many others that went through difficulties but were brave and made it through." Crystal sat a moment thinking of all the chapters in the Bible that contained the stories of other people's lives.

Her dad's blue eyes twinkled. "Just think about Joseph when he was sold into slavery by his brothers. We have the documented account in chapter thirty-seven of Genesis. Through the next chapters, Joseph continued through difficulties, yet by chapter forty-one, he was second in command under Pharoah in Egypt."

"Life sure did turn around for Joseph." Crystal grinned as she looked at her dad. "I guess since I'm forty-five, my life story is at chapter forty-five. No matter how many chapters are left, I know the ending will be great. Maybe I should just relax, trust God, and not worry about what might be next."

"Good girl. That would be the best way. I know it isn't easy, but remember that God never wastes our time or our pain."

"Thanks, Dad. I sure would like to get out of this life without any more pain."

"I wish I could promise you that everything would be easy. Whatever happens, you know I'll be here for you."

"Thanks." She rubbed the moisture out of her eyes. "I'll talk to Olivia as soon as I get home. I want her to get the information from me. And then I'll tell the rest of the family. I want to get through whatever is next. I know God is with me, and He's with Olivia even if she doesn't want anything to do with Him."

"I'll be praying for you and cheering you on whatever the next steps are. You can do this. God's got you, and His loving hands will continue to surround you."

Crystal thanked her dad and drove down Main Street, pausing her vehicle when she got to their building. Katherine had put up the teal and white striped awning, making the front entrance look even more cheery. Crystal drove to the back of the building to park. The little bakery was coming together as her hip seemed to be falling apart.

Telling Olivia wouldn't be easy, and Crystal even dreaded telling Eric what might happen next in her hip journey. He appeared supportive, but she'd noticed the doubt and hurt in his eyes. She couldn't blame him if he pulled away. She knew what it was like to watch a loved one suffer and die.

Good grief. She needed to stop that thought and get her thinking back on an upbeat track. Hard or easy, she needed to keep moving forward because the ending would be great.

Crystal parked in the building's garage. At the sound of an incoming text, she checked the message. Eric asked her to come to his place for dinner. Without replying, she walked to the bakery kitchen.

Olivia stood at the stainless steel prep table, kneading dough. "Hi, mom. Where have you been?"

"I was visiting with Dad."

"Nice. How is granddad today?"

"He's doing well. How about you?" Crystal shifted the strap of her purse on her shoulder. "Have you had a good day?"

"Yep." Olivia's smile dimmed, and her eyes narrowed. "What's up? Something's bothering you."

Crystal took a deep breath and explained what was happening with her hip.

Olivia stepped away from the dough and washed her hands. She stood there scrubbing without saying a word. Finally, she turned, and her face was red. "Why did you wait so long to tell me? I should have been the first to know." She dried her hands as her lip trembled. "You should have told me."

"I'm sorry. I didn't want to worry you if there wasn't anything to worry about. We still don't know for sure if it's anything negative. It might just be a blob of tissue that can be easily and quickly removed."

Shaking her head, Olivia dropped her gaze to the floor, then back at her. "I knew God hated me. First Dad, then Grandmother, then Geoff, and now you! Everybody leaves me. For most of my life, I tried to be a good girl, and what did it get me? Nothing. Absolutely nothing!"

Crystal stood still as tears welled in her eyes. This was not the way she wanted things to go. She didn't want Olivia to get angrier at God.

Olivia's face paled. "I'm sorry, Mom. I just don't want anything to happen to you. I should be supportive." She hugged her tight. "I'm so sorry."

They stood together in each other's arms for a moment.

Olivia gently pulled away from her mom. "We need to put off the bakery's opening until we find out what's happening with your hip."

"I don't want you to wait." Crystal glanced around the kitchen. "Everything is almost ready, and you've been so excited about the opening."

"Mom, you're more important."

"People are counting on the opening in a few weeks." Crystal leaned against the work counter.

Olivia shoved her hands into the dough on the counter. "How can I concentrate while I'm worrying about you?"

"Baking is something you enjoy. It's going to be a blessing for you to stay busy. I need to stay busy too."

"But, what if we find out ...". Olivia scrapped up the dough and threw it in a bowl. "You need something other than surgery?"

"We don't know that. And life doesn't just stop when things happen. Let's keep moving forward and enjoy the journey."

"I won't enjoy it if anything happens to you."

"Oh, honey." Crystal wrapped her daughter in her arms. "I'm going to be okay. I'll get this thing out of my hip area, and everything will return to normal. I'll be dancing again and embarrassing you in no time."

Olivia sniffled and snorted a chuckle. "Maybe I can talk the surgeon into implanting some coordination for you."

"No such luck." Crystal squeezed her tight and kissed her cheek. "You are stuck with my beautifully graceful mobility for life."

# *Chapter 15*

Fascinated at the intricacies of the human body, Crystal stared at the medical posters on the surgeon's wall. How anyone believed we evolved from a piece of slime was beyond her.

She wasn't in the medical profession, yet there was no way a body could function without blood, heart, lungs, tissue, nerves, bones, and everything else being formed all at once. Otherwise, a poor little heart would crawl in the slime, looking for all the other body parts. Of course, when Sean died, her heart did feel homeless and alone.

Crystal shook off the thought. Her heart was fine now, for the most part, but it still did ache for her daughter.

The last two weeks had been so nice as she had spent time with Olivia, her family, and Eric. If it weren't for her stupid hip and the questions of what was next on her medical journey, she would be floating on air.

The surgeon entered the room, greeted her, and asked her to lie back on the examination table. When he pressed on the top of her thigh, Crystal just about came off the table.

"That's where it is." He helped her up and back into a chair.

"But, I thought it was higher in my hip around my hip bone."

"No, the tumor is embedded in your thigh muscle." He sat by his computer. "I'm ordering an MRI with contrast. At the hospital, we have a newer MRI model that will be more clear. After those results, you'll need to see another surgeon specializing in soft-tissue removal."

"Okay. So, do I wait for the call on the MRI?"

He nodded. "You should receive a call in the next couple of days." He also told her that because of the tumor's location, a CT-guided surgery would probably be necessary. If the tumor was wrapped around arteries, nerves, or organs, that became even more of an issue.

She rubbed her throbbing hip. Her life was about to be more complicated than she could imagine.

Crystal thanked him, checked out, and drove back to Crawdad Beach.

Not ready to go home, she drove to the town's park and sat on a bench facing the river. The sun warmed her back as she stared at the water. A cardinal twilled in the branches above, and a dove suspiciously eyed her as the bird took tentative steps toward her.

Crystal knew the feeling; she was feeling pretty tentative herself about what was next on her hip journey. She called her dad and filled him in on the latest. He promised to pray and reminded her to keep the rest of the family informed. She sighed. They were all already mad at her since she hadn't let anyone go with her to her medical appointments. Having someone with her would have been nice, but she didn't want anyone asking the doctor a zillion questions. Because, frankly, she didn't want to think too much about the whole situation.

Hopefully, the tumor could be easily removed, and her life would go on as before. She couldn't have anything bad happen to her. Olivia needed her.

Crystal groaned. Olivia was so excited about opening the bakery, as were all their family members and friends who had adjusted their schedules to help work at the bakery.

*God, I can't have anything wrong with me. Please let it be a nice little self-contained tumor that can be easily removed.*

The thought came: would she still trust and believe God even if the surgery was the start of a long, challenging journey?

Ugh. Crystal rose to her feet and walked the trail along the sandy riverbank. The water flowed slow and steady in the river, and a soft breeze ruffled the changing leaves above her.

God is the great physician, yet some people receive healing, and others do not. What if her tumor was cancerous or would need numerous surgeries? She'd seen the fear in Olivia's eyes. What if God's plan left her daughter an orphan? Crystal crossed her arms over her chest, willing the painful thoughts to leave her alone. She needed to trust God and believe everything would turn out fine.

But that was easier said than done.

Eric stood behind the counter at Doohickeys and tried to act busy, but he kept glancing at his phone, hoping for an update from Crystal. Eric's earlier bravado about not reaching out before she did had lasted maybe fifteen minutes. He wanted and needed to stay in touch.

Last night, he'd taken her to his favorite Mexican restaurant by the beach. Crystal seemed to enjoy being with him and said she loved the meal but still seemed distracted. He couldn't blame her; he was distracted, too, wondering what would happen with her hip.

Crystal's appointment was scheduled three hours ago, so she should be back by now. He still didn't understand why Crystal wouldn't let anyone go with her to her doctor's appointments. She needed someone there to listen, ask questions, and provide any needed comfort.

Even though they'd agreed to date, as far as he knew, she hadn't told anyone. He hadn't shared that information either because he didn't want to say anything until she did. Eric rubbed the back of his neck. They were in their mid-forties, and yet he felt like they were in middle school keeping a secret.

"Eric?" Gloria stood next to him.

He hadn't even noticed her presence. "Hey, sorry, I was just thinking."

She grinned. "Thinking about Crystal?"

"Yeah, just wondering if she's okay."

"Why?" Gloria tilted her head. "Is something wrong?"

He swallowed hard and tried to act upbeat. "Sure, yeah. Sure."

Gloria gave him a look that said she was well aware he was worried about something.

Should he say anything? Even though he trusted Gloria, he didn't want to say anything without Crystal's permission.

Gloria patted his arm. "You don't need to tell me, but I'll pray for her and you."

"Thanks, I really appreciate that."

"Speaking of Crystal," Gloria said. "About thirty minutes ago, I saw her drive toward the park."

"You did?"

"It's easy to spot her Red SUV with the Texas license plates." Gloria motioned out the front.

"Thanks. Could you and Sammie watch things? I'm going to go see if Crystal is still there."

"You got it. Take your time. We'll be fine."

Eric rushed out back, got in the work van, and drove to the park. Sure enough, Crystal's SUV was there. He parked and then walked toward the play area where the benches were located. She wasn't there, so he hurried to the walkway by the riverbank.

When Crystal and he were kids, the path had only been a dirt trail, and they'd spent many summer days walking and exploring the riverbank together. As a little girl, Crystal wouldn't catch frogs, but she loved watching the tadpoles that would swim along the sides of the river.

Crystal was looking down and didn't notice his approach. "Hey, good looking."

Her red-rimmed eyes met his. "Hey." Her smile seemed forced.

He wanted to pull her to his chest and hug her but instead stopped in front of her. "Are you okay?"

She shrugged. "Oh, yeah. Sure. I'm fine."

"No, you're not. What did the surgeon say?"

Crystal stared into the distance before her gaze met his. "I need another MRI."

"Why another one?"

"The tumor might be further down than the X-ray and MRI showed. The next MRI will be at the hospital, and they will use contrast to get a wider look at my leg. I keep being sent to doctors and having more tests. I just want somebody to fix it." She looked up at him, and a spark of mischievousness showed in her gaze. "You're a fix-it guy. Maybe you could take care of it for me."

He got a little nauseous at that thought. "Uh, no. I have no skill in that kind of work. I don't think I could handle anything like that."

"You couldn't be a surgeon?"

"No way. I can handle my pain, but seeing someone else in pain makes me want to pass out."

"Really? I don't remember anything like that when we were younger. I always thought you were a tough guy."

Eric stood straight and puffed out his chest. "Yep, I'm tough. And there was no way I would have let you or anyone else know some things about me."

"Some things?" An eyebrow arched upward. "You mean there are more things I don't know about you?"

He attempted to look suave. "I am a mysterious man. A man of mystery."

She grinned his way as they continued strolling by the riverwalk.

"How is everyone taking the news?"

"They're worried, especially Olivia." Crystal sighed and gazed up at the trees. "I needed to come here just to unwind before I saw anyone."

"I'm sorry I interrupted you."

She smiled his way. "I'm glad you did. Talking about everything with you helped."

"You know I'm always available." Eric touched her arm and stopped her from walking. "Do you need a hug?" He held out his arms. "If you don't, I need one."

Crystal curled into his embrace. "Thanks, Eric."

He held her close, loving how she fit against him. "You'll be okay." At least, that's what he kept praying.

"I believe that too. I just don't know how much has to be done and what I have to go through before I get to the okay part. Fast forward on our lives would come in handy at times, wouldn't it?"

"That would be very nice. And it would be great to have the ability to hit pause when something nice is happening." Eric held her tighter. "I'd have lots of pauses with you."

She nestled closer. "Aw, thanks. I would with you, too."

The sound of a phone buzzing interrupted the silence.

She sighed and stepped out of his embrace. "I better get back before my phone overheats from all the texts I'm receiving."

He stayed in step beside her. "Want to have dinner with me tonight?"

"I'd like to, but tomorrow Olivia is having her first taste testing for the family. She probably will need help baking all the products. Plus, I don't want to be gone every evening."

Eric nodded. "I understand. Just let me know." He walked her to her SUV and made sure she buckled in. "I'll talk to you later?"

She grinned up at him. "Definitely."

Eric stood there and watched her drive away. Every day, his feelings for her intensified. No matter what happened on her medical journey, he loved her when they were younger, and he loved her now.

He just didn't know when or how to tell her he loved her.

# *Chapter 16*

She couldn't wait to hear what they thought. Crystal helped Olivia set her dessert creations on the bakery counter and grinned at their family members and friends lined up for the taste testing. Since it was Saturday, even the kids were there. Olivia handed each person a piece of paper and a pencil. "Okay, I need you to rate what you like best and make comments. Also, tell me what else you might want me to have ready for the opening."

Chester jostled his way forward. "My mouth jets are on full throttle. I can't wait to try your wonderful delicacies."

His wife, Maybelline, rushed up and playfully smacked his arm. "Chester Taylor, get back in line and wait your turn."

His shoulders drooped, and he shuffled behind her. "Kill joy."

Crystal grinned at their playful banter. She did have the best family and friends. Yesterday, when she returned home from her appointment, she told Olivia the latest about her hip. They had spent the rest of the day and early this morning baking everything Olivia could think of, probably to keep her mind occupied.

Even with the questions hanging over their heads regarding her hip, the evening reminded her of the times when Olivia was a little girl, and they had baked all kinds of creations together. Sean had been a very brave man to try some of the things they had created.

Smiles, laughter, and sounds of yums and pleasurable groans came from those who were there to support Olivia's new venture. At the end of the hour, not a crumb remained of what they had baked and Olivia had a stack of papers with comments and suggestions.

His smile wide and his blue eyes twinkling, her dad stood by Crystal's daughter. "Olivia, you have done an amazing job. Everything was wonderful. I can't wait until you open."

"Thanks, Grandad. I can't take all the credit. Mom, Tess, Marie, Aunt Helen, and Maybelline have been a big help."

"You are the amazing chef. Have you decided on the date for the opening?"

"I'm not sure. I want to wait to see what happens with Mom."

He nodded.

"You don't need to wait on me," Crystal said. "You'll have plenty of help."

Olivia shook her head. "No, I'd be too distracted. I'll use the time to keep creating and perfecting what we'll sell once we open."

"Are you sure? I hate for you to put off anything on my account."

"Everything isn't quite ready yet, so it's not a problem."

Her dad laid his hands on Crystal and Olivia's shoulders. "Don't worry about paying me back. This building was a gift. Open whenever you want and whenever you're ready. Of course, you do know the rest of us will be here at a moment's notice to do any taste testing you may need."

"I'm always available!" Chester held up his hand.

Olivia smiled. "I hope everyone likes my baking as much as Chester does."

"Your bakery is already the talk of the town," Crystal said.

"I'll be curious to see the suggestions on what everyone would like to have on the menu."

Katherine joined them. "Based on what you offered today, we will all be thrilled." She smiled at Olivia, then gently grabbed Crystal's arm and led her a few steps away. "I'm going with you to your next appointment."

"You don't have to do that. I'll be fine."

"I'm not taking no for an answer." Katherine leveled her gaze at her. "I'm going with you. You've got to stop thinking you can do everything on your own. Plus, you need someone to listen and ask questions."

Olivia pushed her way in between them. "I'm going too. You need us to help you remember whatever the surgeon says."

Crystal gave them both a semi-irritated look. "Fine. I'll let you both know when the next appointment is, and we'll go together. Maybe we can eat out somewhere fun before or after the appointment."

Katherine took her by the arm. "Promise us."

Crystal nodded. "I promise." She would be grateful to have her daughter and sister with her for the next appointment. She just hoped whatever the doctor shared wouldn't be disturbing.

After everyone left, Crystal helped Olivia clean up the kitchen, and then she watched as her daughter made notes on her computer of the suggestions everyone had made.

Olivia glanced her way. "So far, I need to ensure I have regular items like cupcakes, cookies, and pastries. I also need to offer coffee, juice, and other drinks. One person requested kolaches and baby omelets for breakfast. I could do that. Make a variety of Kolaches and have a fun muffin-sized omelet or quiche."

"Sounds good, but Tiddlywinks is known for serving a great breakfast. Plus, that would be more trouble to add to your baking schedule, wouldn't it?"

"True. I'll have to decide what would be best to offer customers. Baking is my happy place, kind of like you and your dancing. Although my baking skills far outweigh what you call dance moves." Olivia gyrated and jerked as she sat in her chair.

Crystal gave her a mock glare. "Ha, ha, ha."

Olivia grinned. "I'm grateful for all the help from family, but I think I need to hire someone as a full-time employee. I talked to Mrs. Harris over at Tiddlywinks, and she said Jennifer might be interested."

"But wouldn't that put them out a waitress?"

"Yeah, but Mrs. Harris thought Jennifer was ready for a change. She's evidently wonderful in the kitchen when she's not waiting on tables. I'm going to talk to Mrs. Harris and Jennifer this afternoon."

"That would be very kind of them to let you have one of their employees. Jennifer is a sweet young woman."

Olivia nodded. "I like her. I'm thinking about getting a loan for the rest of the startup costs to have money to pay Jennifer and anything else we might need. Granddad has already helped so much, and Aunt Katherine spent all that time fixing up the building. I want to pay Jennifer more than she's making at Tiddlywinks. She won't make tip money, so it needs to be a decent salary."

"Instead of getting a loan from a bank, how about I kick in money to help with your start-up costs."

Olivia shook her head. "You don't have to do that."

"I know, but I want to help make sure you succeed. Running your own business is a big deal. I'm so proud of you for wanting to do this. When you were a little girl, you pretended that your playhouse kitchen was a bakery and that your dolls were the customers. While other kids in the neighborhood would have lemonade stands, you would offer homemade cookies. You always have had a talent for this."

"Running my own bakery is a dream come true."

"It's great to see you excited."

"Yeah, I'm looking forward to this." Olivia's smiling gaze roamed around the building. "I hope it's successful."

Crystal laid her hand on her daughter's shoulder. "It will be. I know you can do this."

"Thanks, Mom." Olivia sat back in her chair. "Today's feedback is helpful, but I need to be careful what I decide to offer at the bakery. Each item could mean the addition of more ingredients. I don't want to rush the process. I need to get a website and social media presence started. Tess is great with artwork, so she'll be a great resource. I'll check with Marcus about a website since he knows security stuff."

"There's a lot involved in this process, isn't there?"

"I knew some of what would be needed, but I had no idea how involved everything was. At least when I worked at the restaurant, I was in charge of ordering the ingredients needed for all the desserts."

"It's a good thing. I wish I could help more. You'll have to give me precise instructions."

"I plan on it," Olivia's eyes playfully narrowed. "Just think of it like when I was a kid, and we baked together."

Crystal got all teary-eyed. "Aww, you remembered."

"Of course. Those were fun times, and that's what got me started loving baking."

"At least I did some things right."

"Mom, you've always been a great mom."

"I love you, Olivia. Always have and always will."

"I love you too." Even Olivia's eyes had gotten watery. She grinned. "Now, stop being so sappy. We have work to do."

# Chapter 17

"Thanks for letting us tag along."

Crystal raised an eyebrow at her sister standing by the examination room door. "I didn't think I had much of a choice."

"You didn't," Olivia said. "We would have hidden in your trunk if you had said no."

Crystal giggled at the thought. "Well, since my SUV does not have a trunk, that could have been a problem."

"Dad wanted to come too," Katherine said. "But we convinced him we would tell him everything."

"It's been hard having to wait two weeks for your appointment," Olivia said. "I'm grateful today you'll finally get some answers and get the surgery scheduled so you can get fixed."

The surgeon greeted them and turned his attention to Crystal. "I've reviewed your latest MRI. The mass is about the size of a softball and embedded in your thigh muscle. We're pretty sure it's a lipoma. You also have a labral tear, and the outside tendons on your hip have tendinosis."

Since she wasn't alone, Crystal tried not to react negatively. "Lipoma means it's probably benign, right?"

"Correct," the surgeon said.

Olivia held up her hand as though in school. "But, what is tendinosis? Is that like tendonitis?"

"Tendonosis is more serious. With tendinosis, the actual tissues in the tendons are degrading. The damage causes disorganized fibers and a hard, thickened, scarred, and rubbery appearance. Tendonosis can make the tendon more prone to injuries, which could cause it to rupture or tear."

Katherine stood near the door with her arms crossed over her chest. "That doesn't sound good. So, what is a labral tear?"

"A labral tear involves the labrum, which is the ring of cartilage on the outside rim of the hip joint socket that provides cushioning of the hip joint and helps hold the ball securely in place at the top of the thigh bone."

"Ouch," Katherine said as she turned to Crystal. "How have you even been walking?"

Crystal rubbed her hip. "No wonder that hurts. Can you take care of all of that?"

"No, first, the mass needs to be removed. I will send you to another surgeon specializing in soft tissue removal. He's an oncologist. After that, you'll need to return, and we can discuss the next steps."

Crystal stared at the man as she tried to process all he told her. How on earth did her body get so messed up? It's not like she had been in a car wreck or was a martial arts fighter. Why couldn't she have some fantastic story to tell her friends, like she had been single-handedly fighting Godzilla or King Kong?

The surgeon cleared his throat and waited until she looked at him. "I'll talk to the other surgeon, and you should receive a call from his office in the next few days."

"Is there anything she should or shouldn't do right now?" Olivia asked.

Crystal looked at her daughter. "I've been getting along just fine."

"You have not. You're always rubbing your hip and limping."

The surgeon's gaze was kind as he stood and looked at Crystal. "Taking it easy and not overdoing anything would be best."

Why couldn't they take care of everything all at once? And why did her hip have so many things wrong with it? Bummed and sore, Crystal checked out and followed Katherine to her car.

Olivia still hadn't said anything, but from her expression and far-off look, Crystal knew she was worried.

When they left the doctor's office, Katherine drove to a Mexican restaurant.

Once they settled in, Katherine turned to Crystal. "You probably need some salsa therapy after that appointment."

"Yes, I do. It's lots to process." Crystal tried to sound upbeat. "But, I know I'll be fine. Surgeons can fix just about anything these days." She scooped as much salsa as possible on a chip and munched away. Salsa therapy was a good thing.

Katherine crunched on a chip. "Now that the building is finished, I am going to start a new project. I'm considering turning the old bank building into a hotel or event venue."

"That sounds awesome," Olivia said.

"That does, but how do you afford to do things like that?" Crystal asked.

"Even though Crawdad Beach kept everything neat and tidy, many buildings had been vacant for years. Three years ago. Michael's dad passed, and since his mom had already passed, there was a sizeable inheritance because of insurance policies. Michael and I discussed how best to invest that money. We both want Crawdad Beach to succeed, and investing in turning the old buildings into profitable businesses sounded like a great plan. The apartment buildings we did are now full of tenants, and I'm sure the bakery will be successful, so what better than opening an event center or hotel?"

"Where would you get clients? It's a small town."

"Our town is bringing in more and more tourist trade, so a cute hotel would probably be profitable. With an event venue, you'd be surprised how many people are looking for places to have wedding or baby showers, family reunions, business functions, and many other gatherings. My preference is that once I finish it, someone would run the business for me." Katherine gave a side-eye glance at Crystal. "Someone who knows the hospitality industry would probably do a wonderful job at either of those businesses."

Olivia turned to Crystal. "Mom, that would be so cool. A little hotel would need a place for people to eat breakfast so they could use my bakery or Tiddlywinks. And an event center would probably need cakes and pastries."

"That does sound fun, but let's get your business off the ground first."

"It's not like the project will be finished in a few days," Katherine said. "So there's plenty of time. I'm still praying about what to do. Plus, once you fix that wonky hip of yours, you can help me with the renovation."

"Oh, so you're just looking for free help."

"You bet I am. You're a great helper."

"Aw, thanks. I'm ready to get this over with and return to normal."

Katherine chuckled. "The surgeon will fix your hip; I'm not sure about making you normal."

Crystal flipped a chip at her sister. "In an abnormal world, those of us who are normal are considered abnormal."

"Pfft," Katherine exclaimed, then grinned and handed Crystal the chip basket. "Dig in my abnormally normal little sister."

The rest of their time at lunch and the drive home was spent in conversations that had nothing to do with her hip. Katherine and Olivia were trying to keep things upbeat. Crystal joined in the fun banter. But, in the back of her mind, the question remained: what would be next?

After returning to Crawdad Beach, Crystal walked to the park and sat on one of the benches. Storm clouds gathered in the distance. The humidity clung, making her shirt stick to her back. The birds were quiet, as though their beaks couldn't make a noise in the damp air.

Crystal put her head in her hands. Every time she met with a doctor, it seemed like something else was wrong. She'd have to wait another few weeks to see whoever would do the surgery. And that surgery wouldn't fix all the problems. Just how long would this medical journey continue?

Why couldn't God just heal her? God made her so He could fix her. Some people would say she needed to have more faith and she'd be healed, that she just needed to claim God's promises. If that were true, cancer hospitals wouldn't be full, babies wouldn't get sick and die, and every prayer would be answered.

Sean had plenty of faith and trusted God throughout his illness. She groaned at the memory of the neighbor who berated Sean for *not* having enough faith, telling him that if he did, he would be well. The man kept saying, "By His stripes, you are healed," as though the verse was a magic spell if repeated often enough with enough volume that God would answer in the way preferred.

Crystal still remembered what her pastor had told her: that the stripes Jesus Christ received brought spiritual healing from our soul's sickness from sin and did not guarantee that even faithful, faith-believing Christians would not suffer or be sick.

Sean never stopped believing, trusting, and having faith in God, and yet he died. Right before he drew his last breath, his face looked blissfully at peace as he gazed up at the ceiling. Then, he was gone.

She knew God was, and is, good, but that didn't mean she liked that bad things happened. The early Christians seemed to understand that suffering was part of life in a fallen world, and they even wrote about rejoicing while suffering. Crystal gazed up at the sky. God knew she wasn't to that point in her journey.

In her peripheral vision, she saw movement.

She turned just as her dad sat next to her. "Hey, Dad."

"Do you have a date for your surgery?"

"No. He's sending me to someone else."

"Why?"

"I thought my hip problems were due to arthritis or something that would need a bone surgeon, so I went to an orthopedic group. Because the tumor is embedded in the muscle, he's sending me to an oncologist surgeon."

"An oncologist?"

"Yeah, only because the other surgeon will be better at soft-tissue removal. So, how did you know I was here?"

"Katherine called me, and I could hear Olivia in the background."

"Oh. They tried not to act worried, but I know they are. I'm sure I'll be fine. I've got faith it's all going to work out."

"That's good, but you know as well as I do that having faith in God's healing doesn't mean it will always happen."

"I know. I was just thinking about that. Jesus healed people in some towns even when their faith was not mentioned. He healed a paralyzed man because of the faith of that man's friends. Jesus healed others when they didn't even ask for healing."

He nodded. "It's hard to understand the difficult roads we travel, the pain we experience, the things we suffer, but we have to trust that God will never leave or forsake us, and He will work all things out for good."

"I know all of that. But what if that good is because I'm dead?" Her eyes shimmered in tears.

He held her hand and squeezed. "It's not death for a believer in Christ; it's a step into our eternal, wonderful, heavenly home."

"I've got to get well. Olivia needs me."

Her dad sat quietly for a moment. "Yes, but Olivia needs God more than she needs you."

Rain beat against her window as Crystal lay in her bed and stared at the ceiling. She kept thinking about the comments her dad had made. She wouldn't stop praying for her healing and believing that God would heal her because she needed to get well and be here for Olivia.

Rolling over, Crystal checked the time on her phone. One seventeen in the morning, and she hadn't slept a wink. The question that kept her awake, the one that kept creeping into her thoughts, was whether she could trust God regardless of what might happen. Would she trust God with her health? And would she trust God with Olivia?

Crystal groaned. Would she release everything into God's hands and trust Him? What if her medical journey was more challenging, painful, and longer than she wanted?

She closed her eyes and drifted off to sleep.

A scream caught in her throat as she saw herself holding Olivia with one hand while her other hand gripped the side of a cliff. Her feet dangling below an abyss.

The kind eyes of Jesus met her as He leaned down and held out His nail-scarred hand. "Let go and trust Me."

Crystal gripped Olivia's hand tighter and held firmer to the cliff. "I can't. If I let go, Olivia and I will fall."

"Trust Me. With God, all things are possible. Whoever loses their life for My sake will find it."

Lose her life? Crystal sobbed and screamed as she fought to keep control of her hold on Olivia and the cliff. She wasn't ready to leave her daughter. And what about Eric? What about the life she wanted to have with him?

Crystal's grip was getting weaker. She couldn't hold on. Would she trust God with her own life, Olivia, and even with Eric?

She looked again at the gentle eyes of Jesus, and the decision became crystal clear.

Yes, she would trust God.

She let go of Olivia's hand and her hold on the cliff. Instead of falling, she floated. Olivia floated next to her. And she couldn't even see Eric floating nearby.

They weren't falling; they were floating in the strong hands of Jesus.

Crystal woke. Whatever happened next, she and Olivia would be safe in His loving hands.

# *Chapter 18*

Gadget, immersed in a puppy dream, growled and let out a muffled woof as she lay on the floor in front of them. Eric had his arm around Crystal as they sat together on his couch. She had shared her thoughts, her conversation with her dad, and even her dream.

"You seem more at peace than you've been in weeks."

She snuggled against him. "It's been a process. I'm grateful God is gracious and long-suffering while I whined, wrestled, complained, and worried. I still don't know what will happen, but really trusting God and letting everything go has been a release. I don't feel like I have to fight for control. I can just rest in His care for whatever comes next."

"You're making me feel guilty. I'm still worried about several things."

Crystal sat up and faced him. "Like what?"

"I'm worried about you. Worried about my girls. Worried about the state of the world. I am worried about being the man God wants me to be. And worried when I can tell the woman that I love that I love her."

Crystal's eyes went wide, and her smile lit her face. "Would that woman be someone sitting on the couch with you?"

"Yes, that woman is you." He stood and pulled her to her feet. "I love you, Crystal."

"I love you too."

Eric kissed her. "I love you whether you are healthy or not." He kissed her again. "I love you whether you are limping or not. I love you for better or worse, richer or poor, in sickness or health." He dropped to his knee. "Marry me."

"Marry you?" Her words squeaked out as she stared down at him.

"Yes, why should we wait? I don't have a ring yet, but I'll get you whatever you want."

Crystal's mouth opened, then closed, then opened again. "That's a big step. Why would we rush?"

"Why not? We love each other."

"We need to date awhile. Get to know one another better. Plus, your daughters are getting married soon. You don't want to do anything to take away from their big days."

"Good point." Eric wavered and had to shift to avoid falling off his knee. "I'm getting a little uncomfortable. Would you just say yes, and then we can discuss the details?"

"Oh, my goodness. This is all so sudden. Eric, I don't have a clue what's going to happen next with my hip.

Olivia is opening a bakery, and we're still trying to get settled here."

"I understand. But I want to be part of your life, be there when you need me, be there for Olivia. I want to have a life with you. Will you marry me?"

"I shouldn't say yes; it's all too soon."

Eric shifted again so he wouldn't fall over. "Who said it's too soon?"

"Um, I don't know. It's just how it is. But if I said yes, would we tell anyone? I don't know how many people even know we're dating."

"The whole town probably knows we are dating. My parents got married after knowing one another for three weeks. Plus, this is Crawdad Beach, and anything can happen here. Just look at what happened with Jeremy and Grace."

Crystal chewed on a nail for a moment as a myriad of expressions crossed her face. She grinned. "Eric, I love you. Yes, I'll marry you."

His knees creaked as he rose to his feet. He took Crystal in his arms and kissed her like he'd always wanted to kiss her.

When they broke apart, they were both gasping for breath.

Crystal fanned her face. "Whew, we probably should not have a long engagement."

He tugged at the collar of his shirt. "Maybe we should elope. You busy tomorrow afternoon?"

She gave him a grin that ignited more heat under his collar. "It's a thought, but our families would kill us."

"True. Should I have asked your dad for your hand in marriage? Is that a thing since we've already been married before and are older?"

"I think you should. I'd love to see his face."

"You think he'd be okay with us?" Eric waved a hand between them.

"I know he'd be okay with us getting married. But what about our daughters and other family members?"

"Not sure on that one. My girls will probably be good with me remarrying. How about Olivia?"

"I know she's okay with us dating, but leaving her alone in that building doesn't make me feel very comfortable. I know it's safe, but still. I would hate for her to be alone."

"Right. Tomorrow might be a little too soon, huh?"

"That would be way too soon."

"A guy can try, can't he?" He wiggled his eyebrows.

"I think we need to take things much slower. I wouldn't want a big wedding or anything like that. Maybe a small service with our family and a few friends?"

"Sounds good to me. Are we going to tell anyone we're engaged?"

"Let's tell my dad first. I think he'll be thrilled. He gives good advice, and Dad definitely knows how to pray."

"I agree. Maybe we can stop by tomorrow after I get off of work?"

"Okay, that sounds good. But I'm not sure how to handle Olivia."

Eric kissed the worry lines on Crystal's forehead. "We can take it slow and easy. I don't want you to worry about anything. Just know that I'm here for you, and I can't wait until you are my wife."

The next kiss she gave him would keep him in a cold shower for hours.

The following day, Crystal still felt like she was floating on air as she stood in the bakery kitchen. She and Aunt Helen, Tess, Marie, and Maybelline were all together as Olivia showed them the proper methods of cleaning the bakery kitchen. Crystal resisted the urge to stand tall and salute as her daughter marched back and forth.

"You are family and friends," Olivia said. "but remember, personal hygiene is crucial. Always keep your hands clean before touching any food item or during food preparation. Always wash utensils and keep surfaces clean."

Olivia handed each person a Rolling in the Dough apron. "Make sure you, your apron, and your workstation stays spotless. After work, drop your apron in the hamper, and I'll wash them overnight. I also have a handout with more hygiene tips. I want Rolling in the Dough to be known for their excellent bakery items and cleanliness."

Olivia stopped and grinned like she had just won the lottery. "I'm grateful for all of you. Jennifer will come over this evening to complete the paperwork to become a full-time employee.

"How exciting!" Maybelline said. "I just love her. You two will be great together."

The other ladies agreed and celebrated the good news.

"I plan on paying you all for your time," Olivia continued."

"No need to pay me," Aunt Helen said. "I love baking and can't wait to help."

"I'm with her." Maybelline pointed to Helen. "I don't want pay either, but I would like one of your very yummy pastries to take home to Chester."

Tess and Marie agreed with the other ladies, stating they wanted to be part of the new business.

Crystal nodded. "I'm here to help bake, check out customers, whatever you need. My only request is a cup of coffee and a nice cinnamon roll or Danish in the morning."

"Seriously?" Olivia blinked and blinked some more. "You all are helping free of charge?"

"You betcha," Maybelline said with a big nod. "We want your bakery to be known as the best in the country."

The other ladies agreed.

Olivia stood still momentarily, her expression going from dazed to amazed. "Wow, thank you all." Her lip trembled. She straightened and cleared her throat. "Okay, let's get started. I thought we could use this morning to get familiar with the kitchen and go from there."

The women followed Olivia as she guided them through how to use the equipment and get familiar with how the kitchen was organized. The following hours were spent creating a variety of Olivia's recipes.

Crystal was enjoying the time, but her thoughts kept returning to Eric, especially about the fact that they were engaged to be married. She was nervous about this afternoon when they would tell her dad. Not that she thought he would say no to Eric, but it still was strange to even think about being married again.

*She was going to be married again?* Crystal grabbed the counter so she wouldn't pass out. Marriage was a big thing. And that meant being with Eric in more ways than just kissing. What was she thinking? No one had seen her without her clothes except for Sean, and she had been younger then. She was forty-five and not as firm as she had been in her twenties. She still looked okay, but marriage meant sharing a house with Eric, sharing her belongings with Eric, and sharing a bed with Eric.

Her Aunt touched her arm. "Are you okay? You're looking a little pale."

"Oh, sorry. I'm fine. I was just thinking about something."

Helen's eyes held concern. "Are you worried about your hip?"

Grateful for the cover for her uncomfortable thoughts, Crystal shrugged.

"Oh, honey. We are all praying for you." Her aunt gave her a gentle tap on her arm. "You'll be fine."

"Thanks, Aunt Helen."

The day passed quickly with all the baking, talking, and laughing. Crystal had kept leaving the room to read Eric's messages since he had texted her several times, pledging his undying love and ending each message with cute emojis and lots of hearts.

Their secret engagement would be interesting. Crystal was pretty sure her dad would be happy for them. But with all the unknowns about her upcoming surgery or surgeries, he might have doubts about the timing.

Either way, she loved Eric and wanted to be his wife. If her stupid hip didn't hurt so much, she'd join a gym and get back in shape before the wedding.

She almost slapped her head; what was she thinking? With her hip issues, Olivia opening a bakery, and all that still needed to be done, she didn't have time for surgeries or a wedding.

When evening came and Eric came to get her, Crystal had calmed down. Jennifer had left to go home, and Olivia had already gone to Tess's house to work on designing the graphics for the bakery menu.

"You ready?" he took his hand in hers and squeezed.

"I'm ready. I called Dad and let him know we were dropping by his place. He's looking forward to seeing us."

"I wonder if he's curious?"

"I don't know. With Dad, he probably already has an idea since he spends so much time in prayer; God probably gave him a heads up."

All the way to her dad's house, Crystal kept imagining different scenarios. She didn't think her dad would be upset with them, but he might try to talk them out of moving so fast.

# *Chapter 19*

His heart pounding, Eric stood beside Crystal at her dad's house.

Henry tilted his head as he looked toward Eric. "Did you pray about this decision?"

Eric smiled at Crystal's dad as he nodded. "Yes, sir. I did."

Henry turned his attention to his daughter. "Crystal, did you pray about saying yes?"

Crystal's face blanched, and she gave him a look as if she had been caught with her hand in the cookie jar. "Well..."

Eric swallowed hard. "Mr. Doss, I'm sorry, it's my fault. I didn't give her any time to think about it."

Henry surveyed them both. "This big decision affects you both, your daughters, and the rest of your family."

"Yes, sir." Feeling like a kid being sent to the principal's office, Eric hung his head. "I should have been patient and waited longer. I'm sorry, Mr. Doss, and I'm sorry, Crystal."

Henry lasered his blue-eyed gaze on Eric. "Do you love her?"

Eric stood taller. "Yes, no doubt. I want to honor, cherish her, take care of her, pray for her, love her, and be with her as long as God allows."

One of Henry's eyebrows raised, and a slight smile tweaked at his lips. He turned toward his daughter. "Crystal, do you love Eric?"

She reached over and took Eric's hand in hers. "Yes, Daddy, I do. I love him and want to be with him."

Henry closed his eyes for a moment as though in prayer.

Eric wasn't sure if he should do the same. Whether he closed his eyes or not, he was praying for help.

Henry's eyes opened, and he smiled. "Then you both have my blessing." He held out his hand to Eric. "I would be honored to have you as my son-in-law."

Happily exhausted after a wonderful evening with Eric, Crystal didn't even mind that she had barely slept because she was so excited about becoming Eric's wife.

She had her dad's blessing, but how would Olivia and Eric's daughters feel? And what would the rest of the family think? She wasn't usually a spur-of-the-moment type of person, and this whirlwind romance might cause a few people to wonder what they were thinking.

They hadn't set a date, but she knew Eric wanted to marry her as soon as possible. She liked the idea, but so many things needed to be taken care of before they just jumped into marriage.

Crystal went downstairs to the bakery kitchen and kept busy helping as much as possible. Olivia and Jennifer worked together like they had been friends in business for years. The excitement between them was electric as they discussed ideas for the menu, items to test and try, what they would need to order, and even went over how to handle the computer system and checkout process. Crystal could see God's hand in pairing Jennifer and Olivia together. Even while working with Olivia, Jennifer talked about her faith in such a subtle and sweet way Olivia never once bristled.

Crystal checked the time. Katherine should arrive in a few minutes to drive her to meet with the surgeon who would remove the tumor. Eric had wanted to go with her, but right now, having her sister with her would be enough. They hadn't told anyone other than her dad about their secret engagement.

The little bell over the bakery's front door chimed.

"Hey, ladies." Katherine stepped into the kitchen. "It smells wonderful in here."

"Thanks, Aunt Katherine," Olivia said with a smile.

Crystal took off her apron and grabbed her purse. "These two," Crystal motioned toward Olivia and Jennifer, "are having a great time making new creations."

"I can't wait to try them," Katherine said. "Jennifer, I'm so glad you wanted to be a part of this."

"I've always wanted to work in a bakery." Jennifer smiled. "And the cool thing is, they already hired another waitress at Tiddlywinks, so they won't be shorthanded. God is so good."

"Yes, He is." Crystal gave her daughter a quick hug. "We'll be back later. Save us a few goodies to try."

"Will do. And make sure you let us know all the information, okay?"

"I promise."

An hour later, the surgeon stood near Crystal as she sat on the examination table. "Based on the large size and location of the mass, there is a chance it could be cancerous, but we think it's probably only a lipoma."

"Why aren't you doing a biopsy first?" Katherine asked.

"Because of the tumor's location, it would be difficult to perform a biopsy. I'll remove the mass and send it to pathology for testing."

He gave Crystal a serious look. "Since you have a softball-sized tumor that is embedded deep in your muscle, you will be *very* sore after this procedure." He gave her a pointed look that left no doubt that her recovery would be painful. "If cancer is present, I'll need to go back in and remove more tissue."

That thought made Crystal a little lightheaded. Hopefully, God would be gracious to let the tumor be easily removed and not be cancerous. She took a deep breath and steadied herself, this was about trusting God, whatever came next.

After the surgeon left, the nurse scheduled the surgery at the hospital across the street from the surgeon's office in two weeks.

Katherine glanced at Crystal as they walked to her car. "You are much calmer than I thought you'd be."

Crystal opened the car door, slid in her seat, and waited as Katherine settled in the driver's seat. "Worrying about what's next isn't going to help. The other night, I had an interesting dream about letting go of everything and trusting God."

Katherine started her car. "I'm proud of you. I know it's not easy to do when surgery is looming on the horizon."

"I'm not looking forward to that, but I am ready to get this thing out of my leg." She still couldn't figure out how a softball-sized thing was in her thigh. She couldn't see it, but she sure could feel it.

"How is Eric taking all of this?" Katherine gave her a sly grin as she drove them back to Crawdad Beach.

"Eric? My friend, Eric?" Crystal tried to act innocent.

"Seriously? You two are the talk of the town. We just want to know when you'll plan the wedding."

Crystal jerked her head toward her sister. Did everyone already know? "Wedding?"

"Oh, please. It's obvious you two are head-over-heels in love. Even when you were younger, you were practically inseparable. I'm glad you reconnected."

"So, if things got serious with me and Eric, you'd be okay with that?"

"I'd be thrilled."

"Really? What do you think Olivia would think?"

Katherine shook her head. "Olivia would be fine. She's a young woman and ready for her mom to let her have her own space."

"You think so?"

"I know so. I talked to Olivia a few weeks ago. She loves having you there but didn't want that to be long-term."

"Ouch. I would feel hurt, but I'm also proud Olvia wants to stand on her own two feet."

"Olivia is now a business owner, ready to make her way in the world."

Crystal groaned. "Letting go sure does involve a lot of letting go."

"If you don't let go, you can't grab hold of whatever God has waiting next."

# *Chapter 20*

**A** rainstorm pounded the windshield of Katherine's car. What a way to start the day for her surgery. Was the storm an omen of what would happen?

The storm made the drive difficult and slowed their progress to the hospital. Thankfully, not many cars were on the road at four o'clock in the morning.

Crystal stifled a yawn as she sat in the passenger seat. Eric had wanted to drive her, but Katherine and Olivia insisted they go with her.

During the last two weeks, Crystal and Eric had spent as much time together as possible. As each day passed, she became more sure of her decision to marry Eric. She just had no clue how and when they could have a ceremony with all that was going on with her medical issues. Fortunately, Olivia had stayed busy baking, having fun taste-testings for family, getting supplies ready, and ordering the remaining business licenses for the bakery and each employee.

Finally arriving at the hospital at five a.m., they went to the surgery department and checked in. A few minutes later, a nurse led them to a room and gave Crystal the not-so-lovely little gowns provided by hospitals to ensure you were as uncomfortable as possible before any procedure.

Crystal settled in bed and pulled the blanket to her neck to stay warm.

Olivia laid her hand on Crystal's arm. "You're going to do great." Her worried expression said she had her doubts.

"I'll be fine. Don't worry. The surgeon will get the thing out of my leg, and I'll be back to dancing in a week or two."

Katherine grinned. "If you're trying to make Olivia feel better, picturing you dancing does not ease our minds. Then again, maybe this will help your dance moves."

"We can only hope," Olivia said with a chuckle.

A nurse entered the room, took Crystal's vitals, and checked her medical information. While she was talking, a medical technician arrived and hooked Crystal's arm to an I.V. As soon as they left, an anesthesiologist came in to discuss the anesthesia she would be given and that a small tube would be in her throat. Thankfully, it would only go part of the way down her throat.

The anesthesiologist checked her heart with his stethoscope, then drew back. "You have a heart murmur."

"I didn't know I had one."

"Maybe you've had it since birth."

Crystal shrugged. "It's probably my heart murmuring that it doesn't want to go through surgery."

He gave her a polite grin. "We'll take good care of you."

After he left, Katherine looked down at her. "We are all praying this goes great without any additional problems."

Crystal nodded. She knew what her sister meant. They were all praying the tumor was not cancerous. Sending up silent prayers heavenward for the surgery to go well, Crystal felt a gentle press in her spirit. She needed to let go and trust God no matter what happened with the surgery.

Olivia moved closer. "I'm praying too, Mom."

Swallowing the rising lump in her throat, Crystal took Olivia's hand, gave a gentle squeeze. "Thank you. I really believe I'll be fine."

The door opened, and another nurse came to take Crystal to surgery.

Katherine put her arm around Olivia but gazed at Crystal. "We'll be here when they finish."

The nurse pushed Crystal into the operating room, and they moved her to the operating table. The anesthesiologist leaned toward her. "I'll give you something to help you relax."

"Thank you. That would be much appreciated."

Before she could think another thought, she drifted into blackness.

Crystal moaned and whimpered; surgery was over, and they were finally on the way home. Never mind that she had been sick non-stop since the surgery. At one o'clock in the afternoon, the nurse wheeled her out to Katherine's car and sent her on her way.

Crystal could barely keep her eyes open from being so dizzy on the drive home and drifted in and out of sleep.

"We have a surprise for you," Katherine patted her arm.

Crystal forced open her eyes. "Whatever it is, thank you. But, right now, I just want to stop feeling so icky."

Olivia leaned over from the back seat and patted Crystal's shoulder. "Mom, please open your eyes."

Crystal moaned and tried to adjust her head to look out the front window. She gasped. Along the sidewalks on both sides of Main Street stood her dad, Chester and Maybelline, Katherine, along with her kids and grandkids, and what looked like most of the people from Crawdad Beach, and they all were dancing.

"It's your welcome home from Crawdad Beach." Katherine rolled down the windows and tapped her horn in greeting.

"Aww, you guys. This is so sweet." Crystal bit back her tears. She waved and tried her best to smile. "Please thank everyone for me."

As the car drove slowly past her friends and family, she noticed Eric holding a big sign that said *Welcome Home, Crystal. I love you!*

Crystal smiled and blew him a kiss. Their romance would not be secret after today. How did she get so blessed to live in such a wonderful town and have the love of a wonderful man?

She laid her head back on the headrest and sent up a silent prayer of thanks to God.

Non-alcoholic Champagne Corks popped all across the room at the celebration that Crystal's tumor was benign. Although the bakery wasn't officially open, family and friends gathered to eat and celebrate, and they even dressed up like it was a formal affair. Olivia had said she had baked all kinds of surprises and hadn't let Crystal in the bakery kitchen for several days.

Crystal was still sore but healing. In another month, she'd have her follow-up with the surgeon to determine when the other parts of her hip could be fixed. She wasn't looking forward to another operation, but she did want to get everything taken care of. She was ready to start her new life with Eric.

They had finally told everyone they were engaged, and the consensus had been very positive. Eric's daughters, who were here at the celebration, had welcomed her with open arms. And even more special was that Olivia seemed genuinely happy for them.

Crystal smiled at the sparkling diamond on her left hand. The engagement ring Eric had bought her, with the help of Katherine and Olivia, was beautiful and perfect. She couldn't have picked a prettier one.

Eric came next to her and slid his arm around her waist. "Happy?"

"Very." She kissed his cheek. "Thank you for being so sweet."

"Me? You're the sweet one."

Olivia shook her head but gave them a playful grin. "You two are disgusting. You need to get married soon."

Eric raised an eyebrow as he looked at Crystal. "I think your daughter has made an excellent suggestion."

"I need to get whatever is next on my medical journey done before we can even think about getting married."

"No, you don't. Marriage is for better or worse in sickness and in health. I'm ready if you are."

"Oh, Eric, I'd love to be married to you this very moment. But there are too many things still hanging over our heads."

Eric let out a whistle, and all heads turned toward him. "Crystal said she'd love to be married right now."

The room erupted in clapping, shouts, hoots, and hollers.

Crystal chuckled. "You nut, I said we still had too many things to be taken care of."

Eric stepped closer. "I can't think of anything we can't do together." He turned and motioned with his hand to the back of the room. "Pastor, would you do us the honor?"

Their pastor, holding a Bible, stepped in front of them and grinned.

"Wait!" Crystal gasped. "Right now? This minute? But we can't." Crystal swung her head around and noticed that Olivia, Katherine, Tess, and Marie were now standing on one side of her with bouquets in their hands. Her dad, Chester, Sammie, and Katherine's husband stood beside Eric.

Katherine handed Crystal flowers tied in a perfect little bouquet. Blinking back tears, Crystal shot a glance at Olivia, who was grinning from ear to ear. No wonder her daughter had insisted Crystal wear her finest dress today.

Eric stood next to Crystal. "We all knew you would wait and wait until you got through the next surgeries. And there is no way I will let you go through another minute alone. I love you, Crystal Doss Baker, and I want to be your husband from this day forward."

Crystal looked at the sweet man standing next to her, the friends and family gathered around and she felt like she was floating in a wonderful dream.

She touched Eric's face. "Kiss me because I think I'm dreaming."

"It's all crystal clear to me." He kissed her slow and sweet, then gently pulled away and smiled. "Are you ready to let go and trust me?"

Crystal gave a quick, smiling glance heavenward before taking Eric's hands. "Yes, I'm ready."


# The End

**of this novel and the beginning
of Crystal and Eric's life together,**

# *To the Reader*

Thank you for taking the time to read Crystal's story. When I started writing this novel, I had no idea my hip problems would become part of Crystal's journey. My character and I are waiting to see what's next on the surgery agenda.

Perhaps you also wonder what will happen in your journey. Difficulties and hardships are part of life, yet we can trust God and release the future into His loving hands.

I hope you have enjoyed the Crawdad Beach series as much as I have enjoyed writing about these imaginary characters. Lord willing, the Crawdad Beach series will continue with Crystal's daughter, Olivia, as the main character.

If you liked the book, would you be so kind as to leave a positive review or tell your friends? As an author, hearing someone enjoyed reading my book makes the long, lonely hours worth every minute. And you never know, maybe the Crawdadians will line the street and celebrate.

# *Acknowledgments*

My sweet husband, Dennis, thank you for all the hours you put up with me as I spent time with my Crawdad Beach friends. Thank you for your love, encouragement, and loving me through all my crazy, ongoing medical journeys. I love you!

Cathy Brewer, thank you for your friendship, encouragement, and the many hours you spent listening and blessing me with your enthusiasm and input.

Patricia (PacJac) Carroll, thank you for your friendship and the fun ways you motivated me to keep writing and finishing the story.

Jack Foster, thank you for the creative Crawdad drawings used throughout the Crawdad Beach Series.

Please visit Jack at jackfosterart.com

# *About the Author*

Lisa Buffaloe is a happily married mom, multi-published author, and speaker. When Lisa's not writing, she enjoys gardening, walking with her husband, and exploring God's beautiful nature. Visit Lisa at https://lisabuffaloe.com

### *Books by Lisa*
**Fiction**
*Crystal's Journey Home*
*Visible, yet Hidden*
*Running to Grace*
*The Masterpiece Beneath*
*Nadia's Hope*
*Prodigal Nights*
*Writing Her Heart*
*The Discovery Chapter*
*Open Lens*
*The Fortune*
*Grace for the Char-Baked*

**Non-Fiction**
*Float by Faith*
*Heart and Soul Medication*
*Time with The Timeless One*
*The Forgotten Resting Place*
*Present in His Presence*
*We Were Meant for Paradise*
*One Lit Step: Devotions for your journey*
*The Unnamed Devotional*
*Flying on His Wings*
*Unfailing Treasures*
*No Wound Too Deep For The Deep Love of Christ*
*Living Joyfully Free Devotional (Volumes 1 & 2)*

# Thank you for reading,

## *Crystal's Journey Home*